The Clifton
Contract

Also by Nelson Nye
in Large Print:

Come A-Smokin'
Desert of the Damned
Gun-Hunt for the Sundance Kid
Gringo
Shotgun Law
The Texas Gun
Quick-Trigger Country
Trouble at Quinn's Crossing
The Seven Six-Gunners
The Overlanders
Ranger's Revenge
The Last Bullet
Gunshot Trail
Gunfight at the O.K. Corral

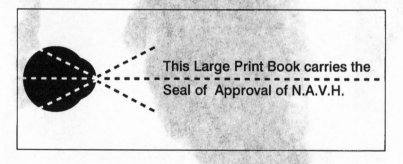

This Large Print Book carries the
Seal of Approval of N.A.V.H.

The Clifton Contract

Nelson Nye

Thorndike Press • Waterville, Maine

Published in 2002 by arrangement with
Golden West Literary Agency.

Thorndike Press Large Print Paperback Series.

The tree indicium is a trademark of Thorndike Press.

The text of this Large Print edition is unabridged.
Other aspects of the book may vary from the original edition.

Set in 16 pt. Plantin by Myrna S. Raven.

Printed in the United States on permanent paper.

Library of Congress Cataloging-in-Publication Data

Nye, Nelson C. (Nelson Coral), 1907–
    The Clifton contract / Nelson Nye.
      p. cm.
    ISBN 0-7862-4811-4 (lg. print : sc : alk. paper)
    1. Murder for hire — Fiction.   2. Large type books.
  I. Title.
PS3527.Y33 C58 2002
  813'.54—dc21
                                              2002031977

DEDICATION:
For my good friend,
DOC KILCREASE

I

They were seventy minutes late getting into Clifton, and the glow from the copper mines shone through the night where Ridge Butler got off the stage behind a Paiute Indian, a corset drummer, and two hardrock men figuring to find themselves jobs at Morenci.

In its more roisterous days gandy dancers had laid a set of rails for a narrow gauge road connecting this place to Metcalf, which had boasted two thousand souls till the placers played out — not that Ridge Butler had any interest in that. By the look of those leathery cheeks you'd have said here was a man not often bothered or even much surprised no matter how the cards fell; but he was bothered right now.

He had a Mitchum sort of face, the build to go with it garbed in sweat-stained hat and workaday range clothes brush-clawed and faded, the rust colored pants stuffed into scuffed Justins. Behind that hard jaw and been-around stare he was quietly simmering, and nothing he saw in this jerk-water camp either pleased or relaxed him.

If that bloodsucking pimp had hauled him into this tag end of nowhere on some kind of goose chase just to put a fat commission in his pockets . . . well, he'd better start hunting a hole to crawl into!

Ridge liked things clean. When he agreed to burn powder he aimed to know where he was at, everything squared off and nothing left dangling to argufy about when it came to settling up. Like all the tipsters who lived off his sweat by lining up jobs, Benny Flores knew this — knew he couldn't abide a hassle of loose ends that could trip a man up or leave him holding the sack — smugly betting the bait would fetch him regardless.

Five thousand clams just wasn't no lure to be thumbing your nose at.

Made Ridge snort every time he thought of it. For that kind of moolah you could hire every bum drifting through these hills. Christ A'mighty! Any number of guys would leap at the chance to snap off a cap for a twentieth part of it; and there were guns you could buy for a handful of silver!

A man had to just about be a plumb idjot — *or greedy as Benny* — to be sucked into anything smelling like this. You didn't have to know who they wanted taken out to sense that this country would be stood on its ear, no more than some fool who laid trigger to finger!

Ridge scrubbed a hand across stubbled cheeks.

Grit from the journey rasped every fold, each weathered crease of that scowling countenance. This frosting of alkali made him seem even older than he felt in his bones, though he stepped down spry enough to have his look around while waiting on his possibles, that quartering glance sweeping across the flushed fronts of the hodgepodge of buildings jammed cheek by jowl at both sides of Chase Creek, the camp's principal thoroughfare.

In the black vault above, stars glinted and flickered like a million winking fireflies through the gusts curling down off the mountain, and his smoldering suspicions continued to gnaw at the turmoil in his head like ulcerated teeth.

By God, that Benny better have some straight answers!

One thing Ridge didn't have to ask anyone. He could sense how they'd figured, looking round for a sucker. Here was Ridge Butler, an exterminating sonofabitch — big rep, sure, but grown old in the business; still a crack shot but way past his prime, reflexes slowed, another Tom Horn too hungry to pass up a chance at real money. Man could bet his last dollar the risks attached to earning that stake stood to heavily outweigh any likelihood of collecting it.

The driver threw down the sack holding Butler's belongings and, shouldering this, Ridge struck out to hunt up a stable, his first need being mobility regardless of what he might ultimately decide. It was a pretty good indication, however, of the way his thoughts ran that — after all his scowling analysis of the prospects — he was still of a mind to have that talk with Benton Flores. If he hadn't been scraping the bottom of the barrel he wouldn't have come all these miles in the first place.

A man didn't have to like a thing to do it.

He'd been cadging drinks and living off loans and handouts more months now than any gent in his boots had the stomach to look back on. But no one who knew anything about him was going to tempt his spleen with any charitable offer of ordinary work. Like with gamblers, pride was the curse of a leather slapper's calling. You had to keep up a front no matter what. Let down the bars and some sneak's blue whistler would damn quick have your name on it.

When he saw the livery sign across the dust of the road on a barn that was still two buildings away, he ran over in his head if the smarter move — in the light of what he'd been got down here for — might not be to simply liberate a mount if it turned out he needed to get lost in a hurry.

Feller on a job like this wouldn't want to leave any heap of bent brush on his back trail. The fewer the contacts made in this line of work the fewer there'd be when the balloon went up to pin you into any given chunk of scenery. More a man pirooted around, more like he'd be to wind up in hemp.

So he went on past the place without stopping. Be hard put, anyway, to scrounge up enough to buy any hide worth the having and then, like as not, it would be someplace else if the need came to fork it.

Take a room at the hotel and sit tight was all the instruction Benny'd put in his note.

Like most of the buildings the Cliff House, when Ridge found it, was neither better nor worse than half a hundred others he had whiled away time in. The room he got after writing 'John Brown' with a copperplate flourish was a second-floor front with a bald-faced window overlooking the street. That this had no cov-

11

ering of blind or curtain made little difference since Ridge wasn't figuring to put match to lampwick. He had all the light from outside that he cared for.

After wedging the room's single spindly chair beneath the knob of the door, he dug into his war-sack and unwrapped the disassembled parts of a high-powered repeating rifle which he handled with the care of an old mother hen. Laying these out on the bed he methodically cleaned and oiled each separate piece of the mechanism before rewrapping the lot, shoving them back in his bedroll. Then he stretched out to wait with what patience he could muster.

Smelter fumes made an acrid stench in the room and the glow from Morenci overlay everything. Ridge was still staring into that curdle of shadows when five taps on the door jerked him out of his doze. He got off the screaky bed with palmed pistol. "Who is it?"

"Me," said Benny's voice.

"Got a handle?"

"Chrissake!" the voice testily exploded.

Ridge hauled the chair out from under the knob, replacing it after closing the door. The newcomer said with an insulting glance, "Sneak up on the dipper

12

ever' time you git a thirst?"

"I'm still able," Ridge mentioned, pouching the pistol. "You're a fine one to talk. Must've caught a real cramp, using up all the words you put into that note."

"Basic rule of my perfession," wheezed Benton Flores, "is never put on paper no words that might fly home to roost." Then said with the lift of an admonitory finger, "A lawyer's first duty is the pertection of his client —"

"All right," Ridge growled. "Who's your client want killed? Phelps, Dodge, or the goddam governor?"

The fat man's eyes jumped about like a sackful of crickets. Each of the three chins above his cravat broke into a quivery shine of sweat as the fish-belly stare came snakily back to fasten on Ridge with a look in which distaste and alarm were almost equally blended. "You have to be so friggin' crude?"

"Let's cut out the gab and get down to cases. Got to be somebody powerful important to get a bounty like that one hung round his neck."

The lawyer, still looking affronted, waddled past Ridge to set his satchel on the bed. With a sulky resentment in the turn of his stare, "I don't," he mumbled, "make it

13

my business to ferret out clients' reasons when they want a thing done." Wind drew in and out of that ruffled face and he was about to say more when something glimpsed in the cut of Ridge's look made him shrug, to say grudgingly, "Not important at all . . . just a ranch owner, actu—"

"Don't give me that! Nobody's going to pay that kind of dough to get shut of some squatter!"

"I didn't say squatter —"

"You ain't said much of anything yet. What's he own? Half the country? This a fight over water?"

"Nothin' like that." Flores shook his head. "Just a average place. Runs two hundred head of mother cows —"

"In this kind of country that's a large chunk of range. Someone found gold on it?"

"Why all the sweat? Why can't you take things just like they are? If there *was* gold on it you think I'd be told? The price —"

"Yeah. That's what's itchin' me."

"Then have a look at this," the lawyer said grinning and, digging open his satchel, began laying out thick bundles of banknotes, Ridge's stare more dour with each added stack.

When Benton Flores straightened Ridge

said with his lip curled, "This guy rob a bank?"

"What are you lookin' so finicky about? I don't seem to recall you ever before appearing overburdened with feelin' in that finger. You been talkin' to Jesus?"

"Look," Ridge scowled, "I wasn't born yesterday! Ain't nobody paying out all that dough —"

"This client is. There's twenty-five hundred here in bills there won't be no questions asked about. You can take my word it's the easiest job ever fell in your lap."

Ridge rubbed his face again. "This guy ask for *me?*"

Flores, rolling his eyes, said, "Ha, ha," without the least suggestion of being amused. "No, he didn't ask for you. I pretty near had to talk myself hoarse! But if you don't want it there's plenty other fish in the same pond spawned you." He started stuffing the bundles back into his bag.

Thick-voiced and grudging, Ridge asked the name of the rancher.

"If you're passing it up that ain't none of your never-mind."

"I didn't say . . ." Ridge began, and Flores swung round with all his flesh quivering. "Either you are or you ain't." The man glared. "Which is it?"

Tugged two ways through a kind of red fog, wanting almost more than anything to tell this son of a bitch where he could stuff it, Ridge stood swollen with rage, inescapably caught between a rock and a hard place.

Every instinct, each screaming facet of Ridge's experience, warned him away from having anything to do with this; but that preposterous price which could well be the last he might ever get hold of was too big a stake to be turning his back on. Six months with no offers had him strapped, beholden. Bitterly cursing behind twisted lips he bobbled his head, hoarsely growling, "I'll take it!"

II

He got up next morning red-eyed and scowling, knowing little more than he had when Benny left. He could feel in his bones he wasn't going to like this, and it wasn't just the price that turned him uneasy. He had the feeling he was being set up for something. Benny's whole attitude, the shifty way the flat slob had watched him — and that bagful of currency fetched down for bait! — all warned Ridge there was more to this than Flores had seen fit to mention.

The spread was Tadpole. Name of the owner C. L. Kelly. Pretty obviously an Irishman, probably scrappy as a crossbred pup.

What was that shyster holding back?

Ridge was still picking at it when he stepped around to the nearest livery to dicker for transportation. Biggest amount of the little Benny'd told him had been parceled out in directions calculated to put Ridge discreetly within gun range of the target. Ridge had his own ideas about that, too.

The whole deal smelled.

Looking over the horseflesh paraded for his inspection, Ridge sourly wondered if this bugger was in on it. Cutting short the burly hostler's attempt to sell him a stump sucker, Ridge roped out a short-coupled claybank with a long underline indicative of real get-there ability.

Ridge tried the horse out after the fellow led him around and grudgingly agreed to take sixty-five dollars, almost double the asking price on the rest of them. Ridge counted out the money, got a bill of sale made out to a name invented for the purpose and, stepping into the secondhand saddle he'd paid another ten bucks for, jogged along the crooked street with eyes skinned for a hashhouse.

He had quite a passel of things on his mind besides hair and hat. There just had to be some damned good reason why Benny's unnamed client would have put such a prodigal bounty on this Kelly.

In a hurry, Benny'd said, "You've got ten days to do it."

"And if it takes longer?"

"If it does you've got all the loot you're going to get."

Flores had said when Ridge showed anger: "I don't make the conditions. All I do is pass 'em along."

18

"And when do I collect the other half of this bounty?"

"When the client is satisfied the conditions have been met."

"I ought at least have a line on this jasper's —"

"The money's in escrow. Already deposited."

"In whose name?"

"In mine," Flores said with an oily grin.

"That's a real help!"

"Client hopes so. You're lucky to get your name in the pot."

Ridge passed six saloons and a couple of dives catering girls and gambling before angling through traffic in the lee of a freighter, got off his horse and stepped through the door of CHICKASHAY JOHNNY'S.

One of the things gnawing hard at Ridge's attention was the problem of where to stash the eighteen hundred and seventy-odd dollars left after Benny's bite and the cost of the horse and the gear he'd bought for it. He put no trust in the mails and wasn't about to stuff any pile like that into no bank; nor could he see himself leaving it in some saloonkeeper's safe.

He damn sure couldn't go loping around with it!

Inside Johnny's beanery four Cousin Jacks and the redskin who'd got off the stage sat hunched on stools shoveling food to their tapeworms. Ridge took the last stool, told the counterman he'd settle for a steak and whatever went with it; and while he was waiting — all through the meal, the weight of that hoard sat heavily on him, finally jerking him onto his feet to drop three quarters beside his plate and shove him streetward without further waiting on that go-to-hell pie.

A cold sweat gleamed along the cut of his jaw. Some two-bit thief could be helping himself to that loot right now and, clamped to this notion, he flung himself into saddle, bucking his way through the bedlam of traffic.

First thing he saw after climbing the stairs was that somebody's fingers had been through his poke. Cursing back of gnashed teeth he grabbed the bureau away from the wall and pretty near dropped it as the breath whistled out of him.

The packets of currency were just as he'd left them, beautifully nested in the window of dust no broom had disturbed in several months of Sundays. Still weak in the knees, he put the chest back and stood braced against it while thoughts like the swirl of a covey of magpies swiftly spun through his head, to be as swiftly discarded. He sure couldn't afford to lose this dough but there was no better place he could think of to leave it.

A look through his war-bag found nothing missing. He slammed the door back of him and went down the stairs, crossed the moth-eaten carpet and then the boardwalk to hitch his belongings back of the saddle. He rode out of Clifton like a man who had all the time in the world and nothing to do with it, dead away from all the advice fat Benny had given him.

But leaving the road at the first deer trail crossing it, he struck out through brush in part of a circle aimed at fetching him into the Blue Range country that lay under the Mogollon beyond Mitchell Peak.

This wasn't the most direct route or the best one but it suited Ridge's mood, being all chopped up in a mazelike tangle of hogbacks and gulches bare as a baby's ass some places, clogged with brush and rock in others, a region that lent itself admirably to ambush. The long-since burnt, crude map Flores had slipped him would have been no good here in any event, and no hired gun with a wheel in his thinkbox was going to risk being frisked with a thing like that on him. Ridge had no worry about finding his man; when he saw Tadpole cows he reckoned by going where these were thickest he would soon enough come onto Kelly's headquarters.

From a healthy distance he glimpsed riders twice as the days wore along. As the hours dropped behind with the sun heeling farther into the west, his mind was kept busy trying to fit pictures to this hombre whose lamp he'd been engaged to blow out. What kind of galoot would a man pay so much to be rid of?

Ridge was in no part of a hurry to come up with him. Only fools rushed in to brace a job blind. Those who stayed in business mostly made it a practice to look over all the angles, orient themselves with regard to their surroundings, study up on the subject, learn his habits. Any plan finally assembled had to take these factors into account, and any gent who figured to be around for the payoff would have several alternate routes lined up for a getaway against the off chance of something turning sour.

Ridge saw no reason for altering a system which had never let him down. Vigilance and considerable care were the only sure routes to survival; waddies too proud to go to that bother were planted mighty quick.

No tinhorn, Ridge aimed to know right where he was going every step of the way. He wasn't out to impress nobody. When he undertook to bring in the bacon his sights were set on a single shining goal — collection of the bounty. He was a staunch subscriber to the axiom that only a chump would ever give a mark a break.

He looked on himself as simply an extension of his employer's will. He was the finger those who could afford him bent around the trigger. No ghosts ever kept Ridge Butler awake. He wasn't the instigator, only the tool.

His name hadn't appeared on anyone's tally sheet since he'd begun hiring out to get rid of undesirables. You didn't learn a gent's habits punching cows for him — not in the ten days Ridge had been given to fix Kelly's clock.

Stowed in his plunder with that taken-apart rifle was a collapsible Army telescope with which he reckoned to learn all he needed. Mighty seldom had he found it necessary to confront a target or even be seen in a significant area by persons having cause to recall his passage. Most of those Ridge had helped on their way had accomodated him by riding right into the bullet that dropped them. Not many unfortunates on the brink of the hereafter, without they were crippled, would stick behind walls for ten days handrunning.

Ridge was a loner with no cronies to betray him. Sure, he'd made a few acquaintances he could bump for a touch — counterjumpers, barkeeps who figured him a prospector down on his luck. The only galoots with any practical knowledge of what he did for a livelihood were parasites like Benny who got him the jobs for a piece of the cake. Killed or apprehended, he'd be no use to such leeches.

While the curl of his thought lallygagged in these reflections the sun fell behind a range of ragged peaks and, presently noticing this, Ridge pulled up to scowl through pines at the deepening downslope shadows. He had small inclination, in country he knew so little about, to press his luck blundering around in the dark.

Hunting a more suitable place to unroll his shakedown, he was nudging the gelding round the shoulder of a spur when the shot slammed a shocking hole through the hush, the sound close enough to move his mount's ears.

Before the claybank could throw any tantrums Ridge was out of the saddle, fist clamped to cheekstrap, head canted to the racket of hoofs rushing toward him.

Twice more the rifle barked through this uproar; and now he could hear the slap of a quirt and the grunts of the oncoming pony.

III

You could be shot just as dead for a goose as a gander.

The light wasn't good but without much choice and no time to pull back Ridge lifted his six-shooter and waited, tight-lipped, crowding his mount against the flank of the spur.

That oncoming jigger wasn't picking no daisies. Barely missing Ridge's shape in its frantic flight the bolting horse went barreling past, a gasp then a scream torn out of the rider as flailing quirt drove them hellity-larrup through breaking brush in a dash for the deeper dark of the pines.

Now, in the swirl of their settling dust, Ridge caught the hammering pound of another and, stopping to consider the foolhardiness of it, stepped clear of the outcrop to rake a look through the gloom.

This second climbing horseman wasn't fifty yards off when Ridge sent a pair of shots crashing downslope. The horse went lurching into a fall, the rider sailing over its head to land all spraddled out.

Ridge swung into leather, wheeling his

mount to go look for the other, sure in his bones that that scream had come from a woman.

After walking the claybank a couple hundred yards he pulled up to listen while his eyes searched the heavier patches of shadow. Hearing the heaving pant of a horse higher up and off to the left he called and, getting no answer, kneed his gelding that way, half expecting to find her yanked off and unconscious.

He hadn't gone more than a couple of rope-lengths when she spoke from a thicket of squatting cedars: "Stop right there. Let go of that pistol."

The voice was tight-strung, filled with tension and danger.

With considerable reluctance Ridge let the shooter slip out of his grip and disgustedly waited.

"Spread your arms and stay put."

Ridge stuck his arms out. In this kind of fix no one but a fool would think to argue with a female probably standing back of a rifle. But he couldn't help saying, "That's gratitude for you!"

"What was the idea shooting at me?"

"Lady," Ridge said, "if you can't tell the difference between a hog-leg and a Winchester no words of mine are goin' to carry much weight."

She seemed to think about that, finally saying, "Back away from that shooter."

Ridge obliged without comment and watched her step gingerly out of conceal-ment. She did have a rifle and the way it was focused put cold bumps along his neck. "I sure hope to Christ you don't stumble," he muttered, watching her come toward him.

"Careful," she warned, stopped above his pistol. With a quick deft motion she scooped it up and, still with her eyes on him, sniffed at the barrel.

"Satisfied?"

She didn't answer straight off but took a long look before presently, tentatively, low-ering the rifle perhaps a couple of inches.

He found it hard in this light to make out her expression but could see plain enough she was still in the filly stage — not really grown up, yet obviously no kid.

She was well put together, dark hair parted in the Mexican manner, hauled back above small ears into a kind of bun that rode the nape of a neck somewhat longer than ordinary, though this may have been the result of her stance, still stiffly crammed with fears and suspicions.

Uncomfortable in the feel of that gun

pointed at him Ridge gruffly mentioned, "If I'd been shooting at you I wouldn't be badgered with all this palaver."

She considered him, appearing to heft that for size. "Sounds like you've a pretty fair opinion —"

"What you smelt in that barrel is the stink of what lifted that rifle waver out of his saddle."

It looked like she wrinkled her nose before she said with head canted, "Your name wouldn't happen to be Lochinvar would it?"

Ridge growled: "What was that peckerneck chasin' you for?"

"I hoped you'd tell me."

"How the hell would . . . Say! You got it into your noggin me and him was *together?*" When she just kept staring, he cried, "Lady, this here's the first I ever been in these parts!"

"Then what are you doing on that Anchor Bar gelding?"

Ridge peered down, then back up at her. She'd have had to have hawk's eyes to make out the brand, dark as it had got now. Must've recognized the animal. "In my pocket's a bill of sale for this critter."

She said, "I'll take your word for it. Choke the horn with both fists and get that horse turned around. I want a look at that fellow."

Ridge couldn't tell if she was implying there wasn't one but with considerable care he did as bidden, not so much bothered by shale-strewn footing as he was about those two guns she had hold of. When he reached the spur's ragged outcrop she called, "No tricks!"

"You think I'm a nizzy?" he growled at her grumpily, and put his gelding round that batch of weathered rock like it was walking on eggs.

In the gloom off yonder he could see the sprawled shape of the horse he had dropped but, hard as he stared, saw no sign of its rider.

"Where is he?"

Ridge shook his head. "He was right about there, in front of that sorrel —"

"He's not there now."

Ridge rasped a hand across stubbled cheeks. That was pretty damn sure! Swinging out of the saddle he began looking for a sign, which he found at once — even where the galoot had got onto his feet. There should have been blood but he didn't see any. Finding it hard to believe he'd scored a complete miss, Ridge followed the boot marks back to the horse and on into the brush where he was forced to give up for lack of better light.

He went back to the horse, bent over, then straightened. He could feel the skin prickle between his shoulders, half expecting any moment to be flung ass over elbows.

"Well?" the girl said in a tightened-up tone.

"You recognize the horse?"

She shook her head. "He can't have got far."

"Probably watching us now across the sights of that rifle! He sure took it with him — and that ain't all," Ridge told her, eyeing the exposed flank of the fellow's dead mount. "Took along some hide."

The girl stepped nearer, motioning him aside. Her face tightened up when she saw the red flesh where the brand had been cut out. "I'll look at that bill of sale now."

But when Ridge dug it up she waved it away. "Don't mind if I borrow that Anchor Bar do you?"

"You leavin' me afoot! *With no gun?*"

"I've got to look for my horse. While you're waiting you can be getting that hull off."

She must have sensed his outrage. Before he could voice it she had a foot in the oxbow, was coolly settling herself in Ridge's saddle. "Here — catch!" she called, and tossed him his hog-leg before she rode off.

He quit looking after her to eye the dead horse. Be no easy chore getting it loose of that kack. Most urgent question in Ridge's mind right then was what its owner would be up to while he was doing this.

Would the fellow try to put more distance between them or — riled by whatever Ridge's advent had foiled — attempt to make crow bait of Ridge to get even?

With a final hard look Ridge bent to his task. It was a double-fire rig, most of the embellishments worn off it from use. His hands felt all thumbs and, smothering a curse, he flung another stare at that dark brush behind him. In this hush a couple birds set up a distant twittering against the early evening chorus being scratched out by crickets. Somewhat reassured, though still far from comfortable, Ridge got to work.

Ten minutes later, with horse and saddle separated, the muted sound of approaching hoofs put a hand beside his holstered iron. As he turned to peer the shapes of two horses emerged from the gloom. The girl's voice called, "You get that hull clear?"

Ridge nodded. "Had to cut both cinches and lop off a stirrup. It ain't going to tell you much."

She handed down his reins. "Better bring it along."

Bridling, Ridge said, "I got fish of my own to fry." After testing the knots that secured his belongings he looked round at her grimly. "You want it, you tote it."

He heard the catch of her breath. "You surely aren't fixing to ride off and leave me!"

"I ain't?" He returned her glare with compound interest. "You think I'm some kinda wet nurse or somethin'?"

When her continuing look was all the answer he got, Ridge, blowing his cheeks out, said resentfully, "Your old man oughta have his head looked at, turning you loose in these hills by yourself!"

"If you're referring to my father I don't have one. He was killed —"

"Must be *somebody* responsible —"

"I'm of age," she said with her chin up. "Anyway, Judge Turlock —"

"You a orphan?"

"You don't need to let that make any difference! If you're in such an almighty hurry hit a lope and tear out of here!"

"Alls I said," Ridge began, exasperated, "is —"

"I heard you the first time. You're quite right to point out it's not your problem if he takes after me again."

Unable to lay hold of any satisfactory answer Ridge, chewing his lip, finally growled, "How far off is your place?" picturing some squatter's shack at the tag end of nowhere or — worse yet — smack in the middle of some cowman's best grass.

"Not over five miles. But you go along. I'll manage somehow," she bravely said and reined her horse past, the whole production, to Ridge's bitter thinking, beautifully calculated.

He had seldom been more hound-kicking riled; would not have gone one goddam step in the wake of so infuriating a hussy if she hadn't set off in the direction he'd been going. When ten minutes later she called back to ask if he'd fetched along that geezer's saddle he still felt too put upon to trust his voice and, ignoring her completely, rode in smoldering silence.

IV

He couldn't even begin to remember any female he had ever run across who so adroitly made him feel a perfect ninny in so short a while. She hadn't looked like that kind when he'd stupidly broken all the rules of action, every precept of his life style, to go to her defense, knocking the horse out from under that varmint in a situation which had no possibility of profit to Ridge Butler.

He'd let the skinned-rabbit look of a scared white face get between himself and the aim of every recent endeavor, the last damn chance he'd likely get to latch onto a stake he might parlay into an escape from his past.

It wasn't enough that in missing that peckerneck he'd endangered his own plans! He'd considerably increased the risks in this deal by revealing his presence to a couple of persons, at least one of which if they found the right chance would be only too happy to throw the book at him!

But a man can't stew in the bubbling juices of spleen and regrets without casting round for some means to strike back. Glowering at that trim shape ahead of him Ridge kicked his mount closer to ask in a grumble if she hadn't any idea of that geezer's identity.

"I didn't get more than part of a look at him."

"Didn't you say your ol' man had been killed?"

"Not *shot,* if that's what you're getting at. A half broke bronc took him over a cliff . . . it was almost two years ago. I don't see how that could have any bearing —"

"Your ol' man knew this horse was green broke?"

"Certainly he knew. No other horse caught up that night. He had to go for a doctor. No one else he could send."

"What'd he want with a sawbones that time of night?"

She twisted her neck in the starglint to peer at him and said on a note that must have come through her teeth: "If you must know, my mother was sick."

"Seems by your tell it must've been pretty sudden." Ridge's experience with squatters suggested that the old bastard — probably drunk — had likely beaten her up and gone too far. Happened all the time with that class of people. Ridge hadn't much use for the weedbender tribe. He said, "What was the matter with her?"

"She was in labor."

When that finally got through to him, Ridge said, incredulous: "Christ A'mighty! Couldn't he count?"

"She wasn't due for another six weeks."

"What happened?"

"I did what I could. The boy was born dead."

Ridge had the grace to shut his mouth after that.

A couple miles later the girl looked back at him again. With more room here she slowed her horse till he came up with her. "Where were you headed when you ran into me?"

It wasn't the sort of question asked of a stranger without the asker had a badge pinned onto him. Ridge scrubbed at his jaw. He wanted her to forget their trails had ever crossed, but since this wasn't hardly in the cards: "Got the halfway promise of a job in the Tonto."

"You don't have to go that far to get work."

"Guess not," he grumbled, "if by 'work' you mean chasing cows' tails for thirty a month. What I got in mind is a cut or two better . . . kind of strawboss job if I haven't been lied to."

After a longish interval of hoof thuds and leather screak, "Don't suppose," she offered, "you'd care to work for a woman."

Ridge pretty near snorted at the picture he got of himself as hired hand to a sodbuster outfit; but he caught back this impulse to tell her straight-faced, "Might get around to thinkin' about that if this deal don't pan out. Uh . . . what'd you have in mind?"

"About sixty a month."

Ridge's jaw flopped like a hoof shaper's apron and his throat got drier than a last year's leaf while he wished to Christ he'd stopped to think before ever he'd loosed those two slugs at that geezer. Sixty a month was gunfighter wages! and where she figured to come up with the moolah was only one of the questions that churned through his mind.

Like a pack of hounds going after a rabbit the things in his head took such a hold on his attention that several horse lengths of travel had been put behind before he sufficiently emerged from this uproar to sense from the half-turned twist of her shoulders she must have spoken again.

"How's that?" he gulped.

She appeared to take a long look at him.

"I said I might even manage to squeeze out sixty-five."

He wished he could get one good look at her face. He figured she must be pulling his leg till she announced coolly quiet: "I'm right serious about this."

Though it didn't make sense Ridge began to believe her.

He blew in frustration. "Lady," he said, "either I'm a plumb idjot or you're outa your skull!"

They moved on through the night with no further sound but the tinkle of spur chains and an occasional screak as one or the other of them irritably squirmed in the leathers. Then, again twisting round, the girl asked, "Why?"

"You don't know me from Adam!"

"What difference does that make?"

"It don't make sense to offer that kind of wage to a feller you never set eyes on before. Leather slapper's pay!" He said with a snort: "What do you figure to get for that money?"

"Protection."

"Pro— God A'mighty! Protection from *what?*"

"Whatever you stopped with that pair of shots back there."

Staring, Ridge had to reckon she might

be bad enough shaken to feel what she paid would be well spent if it served to prevent another go-round of that sort. But her tone wasn't frantic. Didn't sound right now to be shook up at all.

"Probably some saddle tramp. *He's* the one to be worried. Probably lift a fresh horse and keep right on going. Be a fool if he didn't."

"But don't you see?" She kneed her horse closer, caught hold of his arm. "That fellow tried to kill me. If he doesn't clear out what's to prevent him trying again?"

"You got no idea at all who it was?"

He saw the shake of her head.

"You had trouble with anyone? Some neighbor cowman?"

In the starshine the girl shook her head once more.

"And nobody's threatened you?"

She let go of his arm to peer over her shoulder. "What would you call what happened back there?"

Yeah. Ridge licked his lips. It had sure as hell to be either a threat or a damn good facsimile! Maybe this filly had a right to be scairt.

While he was coming to this conclusion another, still rougher, notion began to take hold of him. Two people now — her and that jasper he'd put afoot — both had cause to remember his presence. Both — if he got the job done he had come here to do (and he'd never fell down on a contract yet) — could place him in what the law would regard as the target area.

The thought wasn't one to whip up an appetite.

Maybe the guy hadn't caught a good look at him but this girl, anyway, could identify Ridge — not his features perhaps but his physical appearance, the clothes he had on, the dangerous fact that he was new to this region. If he got in a bind he couldn't shoot his way out of, what this dame knew could put a rope round his neck.

And that galoot he'd unhorsed was in the same fix!

While he might not be sure Ridge could pin the tail on him he'd not doubt for a moment but what the girl could and — given the chance — would.

She was in a bad spot, no two ways about it.

But this wasn't Ridge's worry, nor could any good come of pointing it out to her.

Chewing his lip Ridge rode on without comment. These conclusions he'd reached really complicated things and he had to decide what to do about her. After considerable thought it looked to him like the smartest thing was play along with her, go ahead with the job he'd come to do on that rancher, then get the hell out of this country and stay out.

On their way up a slope he grudgingly said, "Might be you're right. Bird in the hand could be worth two in a bush," and felt the dig of her stare.

"Does that mean you'll work for me?"

"If you pay sixty-five I'll hang and rattle awhile — providin' I don't have to bust up no ground."

"Good!" she exclaimed, and let out breath like a dog flopping down. "You don't know what a load that takes off my mind!"

The stars were beginning to brighten things up some, thrusting their silvery shine through the night. Not enough for him yet to really make out the girl's features, but he could see well enough she'd never have need to advertise her wants in any *Heart & Hand* column.

Abruptly she said a little short of the crest, "We're just about there. What should I call you?"

"Butler — Ridge Butler."

"Any relation to the Karnes County Butlers?"

"Never heard of 'em," he grunted.

"I haven't really properly thanked you, but — what is it?"

Rimming out, Ridge had stopped his horse to stand up in the oxbows on this high point of land and was fixedly staring at the butter-yellow squares of lamplit windows below, at the buildings they shone from — the adjacent sprawl of corrals and stock pens.

The hard, tight cast of his features alarmed her and she reached out a hand, asking anxiously: "What's the matter?"

"That down there ain't no squatter camp!"

"I should hope not." She laughed. "That's a real working cow spread — a *good* one," she added, voice strengthening with pride. "What ever gave you the idea I . . ." The rest died unuttered under the irascible thump of Ridge's fist against pommel. The girl drew back, startled.

"That outfit got a handle?"

"Of course," she said, bewildered. "It's named for the brand — Tadpole."

Ridge's teeth grated. "Thought Tadpole was owned by C. L. Kelly —"

"That's me," she nodded. "I'm Cora Lee Kelly."

V

Ridge stared, stunned.

So here was the reason for that currency-crammed satchel . . . *here was the joker they'd so carefully concealed!*

His bloated face held a greasy shine in the cold awful stillness that towered all around like a wall of stone laid block on block to close him in with the nauseous whirl of notions too insufferable to stomach — like a noose, he thought, spread and waiting.

His fury, the terrible need to lash out, shone like madness in the glint of his stare as the girl's face flinched away from his look.

"What *is* it?" she cried; and the edge of fright in the lifting voice tugged him into an awareness of that shocked stretch of eyes, to scrub the back of a fist across rough cheeks and break his mind loose from the clutch of those visions.

"Sorry," he gruffed with no attempt to explain. "Guess we better get on down if it's your intention to show me off to those boys," and wished to Christ she'd quit staring at him.

She didn't straightaway. He tried to dredge up a laugh that came out more like the squawk of a crow. When she turned away to re-fist her reins Ridge swung in behind down the steep pitch of slope to traverse a dusty lane between pens noisy with the bawling of cattle.

Coming into the yard through shafts of light from the uncurtained windows of cook shack and bunkhouse he pulled up to sit waiting when the girl stopped ahead of him. A hand stepped from shadows to reach for the reins as she left the saddle.

"Jeff, ask Morgan to come to the house." She said across shoulder, "Come along, Ridge."

He got down to scowl after her.

At the gallery's edge she called, "Make yourself comfortable — I won't be a minute," and went on inside.

He saw hide-bottomed chairs on the gallery planks when she turned up a lamp but Ridge, too restive to sit, stood with his back against a post, watching a man come this way from the bunkhouse. He had a burly, short and muscular shape which cut through the shadows with the stride of authority.

"Evenin'," Ridge said when the burly

one, silent, pulled up to consider him. "Morgan? Ridge Butler here."

"What do you want?"

Before Ridge could answer the girl came from the house to say quickly, "Ridge, this is my range boss, Cheeko Morgan." With a kind of defiance she told the segundo, "I've taken Butler —"

"What for?"

The stocky segundo had the look of a man reluctant to brook any infringement of his prerogatives. "I told you flat when I took this job I'd handle the crew. I don't need this feller. I don't —"

"I didn't hire him to chase after cattle." There was a flush on her cheeks but she had her chin up. "I still own Tadpole in case it's escaped you. Butler will be taking his orders from me."

Ridge, while she'd been speaking, had been running a second look over the man now that he'd come squarely into the light. In the blue chin-strapped sombrero, bench-made boots, and cold-jawed stance there seemed an aggressive pushiness about him as Ridge's glance crossed the bristle of mustache to climb up over the hump of nose to the string-held patch concealing one eye.

"Of course," said Morgan, coldly still.

"Muy bien," he nodded, switching to the mongrel Spanish of the border, "but is this man not a foreigner? What can you know of him? What can he do I could not do better — and what is he doing on that Anchor Bar gelding?"

Cora Lee mentioned Ridge's bill of sale. With the downward chop of an impatient hand the range boss growled, "Shackleford —"

"He bought the horse from the Clifton livery. As for the rest . . ." She said with some emphasis, "I know enough," and went on to describe her encounter with the man whose horse Ridge had dropped.

Morgan heard her out with no change of expression. Still with that tone of affront and suspicion he growled at Ridge, "I'll have a look at that saddle!"

"There ain't a thing on it to show who was using it."

"I'll have a look anyway."

With his back to the post Ridge Butler smiled. "Help yourself."

The man's irascible stare whipped to the girl. "I wouldn't trust this feller half as far as I could throw him! You want to keep him around that's up to you, but I'll tell you right now you'll be layin' up trouble. This whole thing smells like Shackleford to me! Who's to say the pair of them weren't in cahoots?"

"But he shot the man's horse — drove him off!" the girl protested.

Morgan snorted. "Would of cut more ice if he'd dropped the *rider*."

Understanding a little better Cora Lee's willingness to put up gunfighter wages caused Ridge to drawl: "You've made your point, Cheeko. Might be you better leave well enough alone."

There was clue to Morgan's feelings in the way his mouth tightened. His breed's swarthy skin took on deepening color as the big fists restively flexed at his sides. And Ridge, seeing the slanch of that tawny eye, hitched a firm knot in the string of his memory never to be where those hands could lay hold of him.

His trail had crossed enough Morgans in the past to judge fairly well how far the man would carry this if he found any chinks in the stranger's expression. The West had a corner on its bullypuss kind, though mostly one found them behind a marshal's badge or backing the play of some cattle baron bent on expansion. Ridge wondered some more about this Cora Lee filly while watching the burly segundo teeter on the brink of letting his emotions push him into some overt act.

But whatever else Cheeko Morgan might be he was not fool enough to let bruised temper take him into a bind. With a snarl of exasperation he was wheeling away to stomp off with his frustrations when the sound of an approaching horse filtered through the clamor of the penned steers yonder.

One foot still lifted, the range boss paused till the mount fetched its rider into light from the bunkhouse. Then with a final snort he moved off.

A peculiar expression compounded of surprise and some stifled feeling not quite so obvious briefly showed in her stare before Cora Lee, lifting a hand, said a little stiffly as the rider stopped before them, "Aren't you finding this kind of late for a ride?" Then, as though conscious of how this must sound, with heightened color, she made haste to say, "I was about to turn in."

The newcomer grinned at her evident embarrassment. "Spoken just like a wife," he remarked with a chuckle, glance taking in the stranger beside her. "What have we here, some fresh competition?" And laughed at his joke as the girl blushed again.

"I'm sorry — guess I'm not used to so much excitement. Billy, this is Ridge Butler, a new man on the payroll," and, to Ridge: "Meet Billy Greene, the man I'm going to marry."

Greene reached down a hand which Ridge, after shaking, thought could hardly be accused of being namby-pamby no matter how easy-going its florid owner might seem. Stepping back he said, "Glad to know you."

Greene said to the girl, "I'll not be keeping you up. Been over to see Shackleford. Reckoned I might as well drop by and make sure everything was . . . you seem a little upset, Cora. Not been having more trouble, I hope?"

She recounted her experience and Ridge's part in discouraging whatever it was the fellow had been up to. Ridge, watching the ginger-haired Greene, saw the man's wholesome face darken with concern. "And you've no idea who it was?"

"Not the faintest."

Greene's glance searched Ridge's face. "Think you'd know this bird if you ran into him again?"

Ridge shook his head. "Was getting pretty dark."

"What about the horse?"

"He cut out the brand."

Frowning, Greene picked up his reins. "Maybe I'd better go have me a look. Might have seen it around," he said, sounding grim.

"Did you get anywhere with Shackleford?" the girl asked nervously.

"Wouldn't even discuss it." Greene, eyeing her soberly, declared: "Cora, I'd feel a lot better if you'd stay out of those hills. At least, if you've got to ride, take someone with you."

"I figure to," she said with her glance touching Ridge.

Greene looked at him again, said abruptly, "Well, good night," and rode off.

When the sound of his horse could no longer be heard the girl, oddly meeting Ridge's stare, unaccountably blushed. Confirming his impression, she had plenty of shape in the appropriate places but, seen in the light from that lamp she'd turned up, there was nothing remarkable about her features with that splatter of freckles and tip-tilted nose. Those hazel eyes — at least at the moment — rather tended to show all the signs of an embarrassing self-consciousness.

She didn't look at all like he'd imagined

she would, with that mouse-colored hair and a smile on her mouth almost painfully bright. With a nervous little laugh she said much too loud, "I think, in the morning, if you're going to be old dog Trey around here —"

"I'm not *that* old!" he growled at her grumpily; and saw an even deeper color overspread the mobile cheeks as her arrested glance, filled with confusion, squirmed like a half-squashed bug.

"I didn't —" she cried rushing into speech and, as suddenly, faltered. "Anyway," she doggedly said, "if you're going to be any use to me, Butler, you'll need to know your way around this country. Tomorrow we'll take a good look at it."

VI

Riding with Cora Lee over the sharp ups and downs of rough Tadpole terrain while the rest of the outfit was engaged with the everyday chores laid out by Morgan, Ridge was surprised to find her so able to converse on range matters and the problems of raising beef for the market.

But get her off these and you'd hardly believe you were with the same person. Whenever he tried to haze the talk around to her run-in with that fellow yesterday she clouded right up, became self-conscious and either would not participate or stubbornly answered with the barest of grunts.

He had thought last night what they'd run into out there might well have come out of the impatience Benny'd mentioned with regard to his 'client' — that the man may have put another gun on the job. Or, more likely, taken a whack at 'removing' her himself.

In exasperation Ridge finally said, "Be a waste of your money keeping me on the payroll if you're going to clam up every time I try to find out what the score is!"

"I hired you to keep it from happening again."

"When I don't know what to watch out for how can I?"

"You were there. You saw —"

"Not when he took that shot at you."

She appeared to consider. "I didn't catch much of a look at him. Jerry started to pitch. I spurred him out of it. We raced for the elbow to get into those pines. All I could see through that tangle of branches," she said with a shiver, "was this shape coming after me."

"Fat or — ?"

"It was too dark."

"You've no idea at all what he looked like?"

Cora Lee said reasonably, "You knocked the horse out from under him. I was frightened. He was clear of the brush when you fired those shots."

"I was tryin' to *stop* him," Ridge scowled. "Never crossed my mind the bugger would be able to get up and slope." He peered at her, dourly. "On the face of it he has to be one of two things. Some ory-eyed misfit or somebody you know."

He could see in wide eyes and blanched cheeks this was something which had not occurred to her. "But no one," she gasped, "has that kind of grudge —"

"Your range boss doesn't seem . . . what about this Shackleford?"

"I've known Orren Shackleford all my life! Morgan's prejudiced; he can't stand the . . . it's preposterous to assume . . . he just isn't that sort — why, Orren's too big a man —"

"Big," Ridge said, "can get to be a habit."

"You sound like Morgan. He thinks just because . . ." Color pushed into her cheeks again. "It just won't wash!" she cried indignantly. "No one could have shown greater interest in my welfare since Dad —"

"What brand's he run?"

"Anchor Bar. One of the biggest outfits south of the Tonto!"

"Big can cover a whole heap of things," Ridge remarked dryly. "How about the rest of your neighbors? They on huggin' terms with him?"

It looked like at first by that clamped line of mouth she wasn't going to reply, but anger stirred by his pecking at Shackleford pushed her into saying with a fine show of scorn: "That's not a fair question —"

"Fair's got nothing to do with it. I can't work for you blind. If you'd rather I got Morgan's slant on the subject . . ." Ridge spread his hands. "Maybe I better just cut my string."

They swapped scowls in silence. But when Ridge made as though about to turn back the girl reluctantly said, "The small spreads resent him . . . but I suppose that's natural; they don't like the way he looks into cow losses. You can't blame him for that. A man has to protect —"

"How do the bigger outfits feel?"

She took a deep breath. "I rather think they're afraid of him."

"What did Greene want to see him about?"

"A piece of range Orren owns. You heard what Billy said. Orren wouldn't discuss it."

"What's so special about this ground?"

"Nothing, really. It's all in Billy's head. He came up here on business and got to looking around . . . I guess you might say he fell in love with the country. Then, after our understanding, he got to working on ways we could make Tadpole better fixed for drought. We've got a few springs and dug tanks, as you've seen, but no running water that's really dependable. There's a deal more water on Anchor Bar; an all-year creek runs through this strip. Billy —"

"Adjoins Tadpole, does it?" When she nodded Ridge asked if the strip had a name.

"It's mostly referred to as the Farley Creek range. Tim Farley having been the original settler."

"What happened to him?"

"He left."

"Sold out to Shackleford?"

That brighter color spreading up through her cheeks, Cora Lee said with a shake of the head, "Orren acquired it from Ed Spaulding, the man Farley sold to."

Ridge, thoughtfully weighing her choice of words, asked, "How long did this Spaulding hang onto the place?"

She caught his thought and told him, frowning, "It wasn't like that. Orren offered Spaulding a chance to double his money."

"How long?"

She said, half angry, "Three or four months. But you're barking up the wrong tree if you think —"

"I thought this was all open range around here, a 'free grass' country," Ridge cut in.

"The most of it is."

"All a man has, then, all that he could put on the market is whatever 'improvements' he's put onto what little ground he's taken patent to?"

"Well . . . I suppose so."

"Actually, of course," Ridge guessed, thinly smiling, "it doesn't work out to be quite that equitable. Big outfits generally cut a country up between them. Spreads not big enough to look out for their rights havin' to take whatever's left over. Ain't that about the size of it?"

It was plain she didn't much relish such bluntness. But she was honest enough to grudgingly nod.

"So," Ridge said, still with that sardonic flash of teeth, "why doesn't this helpful Shackleford hombre pass you an invite to share Farley's creek?"

Chin up, cheeks flushed, she stared straight ahead.

"Ain't he that good a friend?"

"*Now* you sound like Billy!" she cried.

"Well, why else would Greene be offerin' to buy . . ."

"I told you! He came up here to buy. He wants —"

"Up from where?"

"Don't you take *any*one at face value?"

"I'd take you if —"

She gave him a hard look. "I'm already spoken for. Billy Greene's got a head on his shoulders. He saw straightaway —"

"You said he came up here. Up from where?"

58

"Florida. It wasn't till after we got engaged that —"

"What kind of business was he in down there?"

"Cattle. He owns the Boxed Bell near Kissimmee —"

"I've heard of it," Ridge nodded. "I'd think Boxed Bell was range enough for anyone. What's he want with Farley Creek?"

"I've already told you. He figures Tadpole in a time of bad drought would stand a lot better chance —"

"I got that part. What I don't see is what fetched him up here out of that lush country for hunting range in the first place. Or how come he picked this place."

The girl said, bristling: "Why don't you ask him?"

"Might just do that," declared Ridge, chuckling, watching the come-and-go color of tightened cheeks.

There was a heap of vitality stored in this girl and he reckoned it a pity she didn't let it show more. Seemed almost like she was afraid or ashamed of it. He found himself wondering what she'd be like in bed.

Watching the angry look of her go loping off, admiring the graceful swing of her body, he considered the possible facts he'd tugged out of her. Neither of the men she'd probably ask for advice appeared to have a very high opinion of the local Mr. Big.

Cattle barons, in Ridge's experience, generally ran pretty much to a pattern. The big got bigger while the small got children. If Shackleford truly had put on his Sunday manners Cheeko Morgan and this swamp country beau could well be right in suspecting his motives. As Ridge had already pointed out, if Anchor Bar's owner, well bedded in water, wanted really to be helpful why hadn't he offered her the use of that creek?

Catching up he asked without going all around Robin Hood's barn: "Ever seemed to you like this feller Orren might be leanin' toward matrimony?"

Her face came around with a look of complete astonishment. "Orren Shackleford's old enough to be my father!"

"You don't have to get your back up. I never run across no big auger yet that would stick out his tongue at a chance to get bigger. Wouldn't be the first time December courted June."

Her cheeks blazed again. Fire flashed in the eyes above that splatter of freckles. She said abruptly, plainly resentful, "I think we'll go over. You could do with a look at him."

VII

Ridge Butler, about the time he'd begun to get dry behind the ears, had learned how much store a man should set on appearances. Though the habiliments of grace and other respected attributes were frequently donned by persons quite apt to be stopped at the Pearly Gates, if a man's environment meant anything at all there must, he judged, be a considerable streak of vanity in the cowman Cora Lee called Orren.

A lot of whitewash and red tiled roofs had gone into the making of what lay spread out before them. Anchor Bar headquarters inclined Ridge to feel like pinching himself as he took in the trees and quiet beauty around him, the flowering shrubs, the lack of litter, the stout corrals and dozen penned horses in prick-eared attention watching their approach.

The girl laughed at Ridge's expression. "Well?" she said with a faint touch of malice.

"Chipper as a coop full of catbirds," he grunted. Then, grinning back at her, "Sure hurts a man's eyes to think of the folks this geezer has squeezed to afford all the fooforaw he's got around here."

The girl considered him while tightening cheeks put a rim of thinner color about her mouth. Before she laid hold of satisfactory words a hand, stepping out of the nearest barn as some of the penned horses set up a nickering, flipped up his head, blinked and swung toward them.

Whatever Cora Lee had been fixing to say Ridge reckoned she would likely get back to it later — she had that glittery look in her eye.

"Mr. Shackleford around?" he called, shifting weight.

"Try the house," the man waved, and wheeled to head corralwards. But in midstride stopped to call over a shoulder, "Want I should take care of them horses, Miz Cora?"

"We won't be here that long," Ridge answered, and kneed his mount toward the pepper-tree shaded verandah, hearing the sounds of her following horse.

Swinging down he dropped reins to reach up but she got off by herself, ignoring his hand. The screen door pushed open and a man's deep voice said, "What a pleasant surprise. Welcome to Anchor Bar.

How are things with you, Cora?"

"Well enough, I guess."

"Come in — come in." He held open the door.

"We can't stay," she said, returning his smile. "I'm showing a new man around the country. Orren, shake hands with Ridge Butler."

Letting go of the door, Shackleford stepped forward, a small graying man with a grip firm and dry who, looking Ridge over with a quick probing glance, said casually, "Your friend, Greene, don't seem to care how he spends money." When the girl looked puzzled: "Came over here yesterday trying to buy that Farley Creek range — didn't seem to want to take no for an answer."

Cora Lee laughed. "Billy's bound and determined we're in for a drought. He doesn't put much faith in springs and dug tanks."

"He was figuring to buy it for you? Shucks," Shackleford said with a chiding look, "you can use that water any time you've a mind to — guess I took it for granted you would know that, Cora. After all the years your Dad and . . . ."

"It was Billy's idea, not mine," she explained with a gray-green vindicated look at Ridge. "I suppose this country must seem terribly dry to him."

"Yes. Well," Shackleford said with nothing but friendly concern on his face, "I trust we've got that straightened out now. Your critters are welcome to water there anytime. I'm glad you came by. Sure you can't stop and set a spell?"

"We really must go."

When the girl turned away the ranchman, glance touching Ridge in idle curiosity, came off his veranda to walk after them and stop with a hand against the claybank's hip as Cora Lee, fisting her reins, swung up.

"See you favor a Sharps," he mentioned, eyeing the scabbarded rifle Ridge had put together only that morning. "Do much hunting?"

"I don't often get the chance anymore." Ridge said soberly, "I'd a reason for packin' that iron this morning," and looked at the girl. "You ought to tell him what you run into yesterday."

Watching Shackleford while she recounted the frightening experience, he saw nothing but an angered concern in that stare. "Things have come to a fine pass in this country when a woman's not safe to ride around by herself!" the Anchor Bar owner exclaimed in riled tones.

Ridge got into his saddle as the man stepped back. "Understand you been losing a few cows off and on."

Shackleford's angry look swept his face. "Think it's some of that trash?"

"I'm too new to these parts to be making wild guesses."

"My sentiments," Shackleford said, "are too well known for these loose rope and cinch ring artists to take any chances if it looked like Cora might run into something. You been back there this morning?"

She lifted tired shoulders and let them fall. "Too busy."

"Maybe we ought to take another look round," Shackleford proposed. "If you can wait till I get on a horse I'll go with you."

"Not much use."

And Cora Lee said, "He won't be there now."

Nursing a scowl the ranchman nodded. "Sounds a pretty cool customer laying off to cut that brand from his horse." His look swung to Ridge. "You find his brass?"

"Too dark. Must of fired from the brush, and that's where he took that hide — back of it. Man on foot wouldn't leave much sign in that kind of country."

The small man rubbed at the side of his chin. "You've a good eye for horseflesh," he observed with his look running over the claybank.

"I've rode worse," Ridge admitted. "Surprised you would part with him."

"You can't keep 'em all."

"Well," Cora Lee asked when they had got out of earshot, "what do you think?"

"Seemed friendly enough."

"That the best you can do?"

"Can't hardly pass judgment on a feller just met."

"You heard him say we can use that water —"

"You had him in a corner. I'll say this much though. He sure didn't waste no time gettin' out of it."

The girl's darkening stare beat against his face. A touch of impatience was in the cant of her jaw, and with that scowl round her mouth some of this came through her voice when she declared, "I'd purely hate to someday find I'd as poor an opinion of folks as you!"

Butler, grunting, took a hitch on the impulse that was cramming brash words against the backs of his teeth, growling, "When you get shed of them blinders you may find being grown up —"

"I'm grown up now!"

His derisive grin sent hot flags of color pounding into her cheeks and that angry look was noticeably heightened when he said with a snort, "Man would think in that case you'd be showin' more savvy."

"About what?"

"The kind of bind you been put in."

She peered a long time at him before saying, "I wasn't aware of being in a bind —"

"What'd you want with me then? Without there's some grudge you ain't told me about, any kid in three-cornered pants would've figured somebody's got their sights on this spread of yours."

She looked a bit startled, her eyes turning thoughtful as their horses continued to put ground behind them. "Where'd you get hold of that preposterous notion?"

"Nobody's goin' to take a shot at a woman without there's something he wants powerful bad."

She continued the wide-eyed search of his face. "Are you trying to frighten me?" When she got no change out of that she protested, "But what you're implying just doesn't make sense!"

"No one's made you an offer?"

Her eyes came unfocused, passing through and beyond him, sharpening to grapple some new thought she'd caught sight of. Her shoulders stirred with impatience as though to shake it away.

Ridge said, "Who was it?"

She shook her head. "It wasn't like that."

Ridge said impatiently: "We're not playin' drop the handkerchief, Cora! I saw the mark of that slug on your saddlehorn. Whoever it was took that shot at you yesterday is playin' for keeps."

Though her cheeks had paled she couldn't believe it.

"Killing me wouldn't get him Tadpole."

"I sure wouldn't bank on it. Who made you the offer?"

She shook her head.

"Not much point to my stickin' around if —"

"I haven't had any offers. All he said was," she grudgingly admitted, "if I ever decided to put the ranch on the market he'd like first chance at it."

"Put a name to him," Ridge said, but she looked straight ahead and the rest of the trip was unraveled in silence.

As they rode into Tadpole's yard an hour and a half later he made one final try. "At least tell me how long it's been —"

"About two weeks," she said shortly and, quitting the saddle, went into the house.

VIII

After rubbing both horses down, Ridge turned them loose with the stock in the day pen, slid the bars back in place and, warned by sounds of the returning crew, struck out for the bunkhouse to scrub up for grub call.

He was remembering how the Anchor Bar owner had scrutinized the scabbarded Sharps on his saddle — that taken-apart rifle he'd fetched out of sight among the cherished store of possibles he still lugged around through the ten lonely years he'd been plying his trade. As he pulled up his glance that narrowing stare encountered his things piled on the stoop with Cheeko Morgan, lounging just back of them, blocking the door.

Ridge took in that muscular sleeve-rolled shape from bench-made boots with their fancy stitching on up past the sneering mouth to the tawny eye above the bristling mustache, dropping back to scan again the glint of green bola securing the straps of the blue sombrero beneath Morgan's cold-jawed outthrust chin.

The quiet increased as the crew fanned

out in a kind of half circle behind the new hand to watch, some with grins as they looked from the man to his moved-out belongings.

The prospect of trouble was a tangible smell in this fading light as Butler without any change of expression picked up his cue to casually ask, "Your idea, Cheeko?"

"No room inside — no room for you, either."

"Thought Miz Cora seemed to have other notions."

Grinning, lips thin and crooked, the range boss said, "*I'm* runnin' Tadpole. I don't want you around."

"Guess that's clear enough. Mind saying why?"

Morgan scratched his back between broad shoulders against the jamb of the door, that wind-ruddied face turned visibly hostile, while the tawny eye not covered by the patch showed brighter and strengthening evidence of antagonism.

"You come in here on a Anchor Bar horse with all the earmarks of a Shackleford gunnie. This evenin' you took Cora over there. How much is he payin' you to lean on this crew?"

"Today's the first time I ever laid eyes on him —"

"All who believe that can stand on their heads. Now pick up your duffle and hit the trail."

Ridge leisurely turned and surveyed the man's crew, mind evenly balanced between Morgan's order and several possible alternatives. Finally shrugging he moved toward the stoop and his stacked-up possessions, bending over the planks to reach for the sack the man had emptied them out of. With a sneer on the mouth beneath that bristling mustache Morgan kicked it toward him . . . and came down with a resounding bone-jarring thump. Still hanging onto the boot he'd grabbed hold of Ridge, stepping back, dumped the wild-eyed segundo ignominiously into the dust.

Someone gasped back of Ridge and Morgan's upstaring face became apoplectic. Such a wildness was in him with his hands looking on he clawed for his pistol and would doubtless have used it had the swing of Ridge's boot not torn it from his grasp.

He came off the ground in a slashing leap, slamming into Ridge with a meaty impact. Breath belched from both men and, as Ridge staggered back, Morgan tried to get those thick arms locked about him. Grunting, wheeling, fiercely plunging, Ridge drove a knee up between the man's legs and threw him off.

A shuddery scream ripped from that gone-white, twisted face as Cheeko Morgan sprawled in the dust, both fists clutched to his agonized parts. Ridge stood over him breathing hard and with a panting grunt yanked Morgan upright and struck him again. Morgan's face turned red as blood gushed out of his battered nose. Ridge hit him once more and turned him loose and the man fell rubber-legged against the stoop planks.

Butler's still bleak stare kept tab on Morgan till the Tadpole boss, groaning, stirred and came round to push himself up off the splintery boards. Ridge said then in a flat controlled tone, "Pick up my stuff and put it back where you got it."

It looked for a moment as though the man was about to take another whack at it; but the impulse weakened and he drew the back of a fist across mashed lips and went brittly round gathering up Ridge's things and stuffing them gloweringly into the sack he had emptied them out of.

When he finally straightened, "Tote it back inside," Ridge said and, ignoring Morgan, had his look at the rest of them still in the saddles. "So you'll know where we stand, someone took a shot at Miz Kelly last evening. I happened to be near enough to knock down his horse but the man's still at large and she's payin' gun wages for me to keep him away from her."

With a hard slanching stare he picked up his Sharps, wheeling back toward the day pen where he roped a fresh mount and — not waiting on supper — climbed aboard and rode off.

The night and his thinking were about of a color. Though not too much bothered by his set-to with Morgan, he knew well enough no vinegaroon of Cheeko's stripe would be taking much rest till he'd found some means of evening the score. He'd face to make up in the sight of his crew and, without he could do it, he might just as well cut his string and pack out.

A lot more worrisome in Ridge's view of things was the job he'd taken that down-payment for. Even were Ridge at all minded to do so Benny'd never in this world agree to let him give it back. Peckerneck bastard couldn't stay in business if he let a hired gun pull that sort of shenanigan.

There wasn't any one thing Ridge could

pin his vile mood on. The whole combination of things he'd done here from the time he'd accepted that satchelful of banknotes to that damn fool performance with Cora Lee's range boss could hardly be considered to have been in his best interests. Any galoot who hadn't lost half his marbles ought to've known better than go tearing into whatever that ranny'd had in mind for Cora Lee.

Now the whole Tadpole crew knew what he looked like!

The only thing in his favor Ridge was able to extract from the treadmill of notions tramping through his noggin was that when somebody found her dead of lead poisoning they might not straightaway attempt to lay it at the door of the stranger she had hired to protect her.

One thing at least was plain as plowed ground. If she was found knocked off by any slug from a Sharps he'd have about as much chance as a wax cat in hell!

He guessed if he were halfway smart he'd go pick up that goddam stake and keep right on a-riding. Before Benton Flores and his client woke up he could be clean across the Mexican border. . . .

IX

Time he got his next look at Clifton a rimming of pink had come into the east where
the sky's dark bowl met the thrust-up black
contours of sentinel mountains, and Ridge
was less inclined to haul his freight than
when the notion had first latched onto him.

For one thing Benny in the grip of emotions too cogent to resist was practically
certain to prod up a search and, if this
didn't get back those bundles of banknotes, the shyster was capable of cooking
up something which would set all the
hounds of the law to baying. Flores could
manage this with very little likelihood of
repercussions — you could always trust
Benny to cover his *own* tracks. A handful of
details anonymously siphoned to the
proper authorities would put dead-or-
alives out for Ridge in short order, and
once that happened there'd be no turning
back.

Twenty-five hundred, even south of the
Border and frugally hoarded, was not calculated to last out the days of a man still
hearty at age 32, even if the bounty

hunters failed to get at him.

There had to be a better way to beat this than running, and he went over the more probable angles once again. The Sharps was out — he'd be a fool to use it now. There were a heap of other ways that stupid girl could be got rid of. Accidents happened every day of the year and he guessed he could rig something good enough to pass. But he'd a strong urge first to make sure that dinero was still where he had left it.

It was considerably lighter in the east when he dropped into the canyon and put the Tadpole gelding between the rows of business houses flanking Clifton's crooked street.

Threading his way through a procession of freight rigs he pulled up at the rack of the first beanery he came to and sat down at the counter to make up for the meal he had missed last night. It was surprising what a pack of folks were already out and feeding their faces. He was still more surprised while finishing his pie to look up and find Billy Greene plopping down next to him.

Greene jerked a nod. "What are you doing here? Thought Cora hired you to dig out that feller —"

"I'm workin' on it," Ridge said, getting out the makings.

Cora Lee's intended gave the biscuit shooter his order; then Ridge asked, "What's your impression of this Shackleford hombre?" Greene said with a shrug, "Haven't been much around him."

"When you talked to him about that Farley Creek range —"

"He figures to hang onto it. Made that plain enough."

Ridge fired his hand-rolled, watched the blue smoke drift out over the counter. "Think he could be trying to get his claws into Tadpole?"

Greene's look turned thoughtful. With his hat on the rack the roan dimensions of neatly trimmed mustache and carefully brushed curly hair gave the man in those clothes of a prosperous cattleman the suavely persuasive aura of one who has spent much time on the boards. Even his bold good looks seemed to border on being just a little theatrical.

The blue eyes lit up with a twinkle as he caught the studying look on Ridge's face. "Do I pass?" he asked with the whimsical grin of the man who has everything. "Always pays to shape up to watchdogs and rich widows."

Ridge grudgingly smiled. Wasn't hard to see how a man with Greene's advantages and cool assurance would sweep a kid like Cora right up off her feet. "You still haven't answered the question," he grunted.

Greene said in his easy teasing way, "I've not seen any evidence of such an intention. Ever take a good look at that one-eyed Morgan?"

"What about him?"

"Don't it seem queer to you that a foreman with Cora's best interests at heart hasn't seen the need to get hold of more water?"

"Who says he hasn't?"

"When I first brought up that Farley Creek range, suggesting to Cora that she ought to acquire it, Morgan shrugged off any need for expansion. Claimed her dead daddy hadn't seen any likelihood of Tadpole cows suffering. Said those springs hadn't gone dry yet."

"He hold that job under Cora's old man?"

Greene nodded. "I've sometimes thought from his looks he might have been contemplating marrying that property."

Ridge stubbed out his smoke. "You don't reckon he's the one took that shot at her?"

"I'll say this much. Behind his bad manners," Greene replied through a frown, "that feisty son has a lot more ambition than he's given credit for. *If* he's been nursing any fond delusions of one day being the owner of that spread how could he miss its biggest lack?" Head dipping toward Ridge, Greene said in lowered voice: "I've made it a point to find out a few things. The old man eight years ago was forced to unload several carloads of steers at a giveaway price when a siege of dry weather nearly sent him up the spout."

"Perhaps Cheeko wasn't working for Tadpole then."

"I can't say who he was working for but his name's on the pay-sheets." Greene said darkly, "As a common hand."

Ridge's lifted glance swept the cowman's face.

"If this Anchor Bar mogul was such a pal of Kelly's why didn't Cora's old man water his stuff at Farley's creek — or didn't Shackleford control it then?"

"He controlled it all right. Maybe Kelly was too proud or bullheaded to ask. Or he might have kept figuring that drought couldn't last — might've had other reasons. Seems he wasn't the sort to take advice comfortably."

Ridge, sifting this through his head, asked dryly, "In your coyotin' round did you find out who took them steers off his hands?"

"Friend Orren." Greene smiled.

Cora's intended wasn't nobody's fool, Ridge reflected as the screen swung behind the fellow's departure. Man could do a heap worse than take a page from his book, Ridge thought, holding up his cup to get the cook's attention.

When he got it refilled Ridge sat on a while, thoughtfully staring through the steam coming off it. Greene hadn't appeared to think too highly of Morgan, as a man or cow boss either; and there was apparently no love lost between him and Shackleford, though his references to the latter were enigmatic enough to whet Ridge's interest. He wished there was some way he could make sure whether or not Orren had thought to marry Cora. If a man had more time . . .

Billy Greene's assumption that Morgan had been nursing such an ambition appeared not too unreasonable on a number of counts, but was there any real basis for suspecting the Tadpole segundo of being a Shackleford understrapper?

On the face of things this did not seem likely; yet thieves, Ridge reminded himself, had fallen out before. It was hardly conceivable the pair had been partners. But this did not preclude Morgan's having been in Shackleford's pay; and if Cheeko had figured he might annex Tadpole through double harness he seemed scarcely the kind to let any arrangement with Anchor Bar stop him.

And what of handsome Billy Greene, this cowman from Florida who'd stepped in to sweep the plans of that other pair into the trash heap? If either or both had hoped to marry the spread Cheeko certainly, upon learning the prize had been snatched from his reach, would be — from what Ridge had seen of him — enraged enough to try just about anything. Yet wouldn't he, Ridge reasoned, be more apt to attempt Greene's destruction than eliminate the goose he'd thought might hatch his golden eggs?

Greene wouldn't want her dead on any count and Shackleford, even if bent on expansion, surely had better sense than attempt to take over the range and stock of a girl killed by gunshot.

The likeliest prospect was certainly Morgan.

Perhaps Cheeko figured to frame her removal onto somebody else. To so arrange things once he was rid of her that some faked 'proof' or considerable suspicion would implicate either Anchor Bar's owner or the man who was betrothed to her.

Yet, while the Tadpole segundo might be cunning enough to shift the blame to someone else's doorstep, where would he find the bagful of loot Benny'd dumped on Ridge's bed to set him up for this caper? And *if* Cheeko'd done this why risk tipping the applecart with that hit and scoot business Ridge himself had aborted?

Nothing about this deal made sense; and least of all could Ridge believe the owner of that horse he had dropped was nothing more than some raunchy drifter. Fellow might be a hired gun but deep in his bones it was Ridge Butler's hunch the galoot who had squeezed off that shot at Cora just about had to be Benny's client.

X

The lawyer worked out of Dallas and had come a far piece to set up this job and put that satchelful of dollars in Ridge's hands. Although the man had a real lust for money it must have taken more than just the usual commission to move that fat slob by train and stage all those miles to the rendezvous at Clifton. No ordinary client could have put that shyster to any such amount of inconvenience and discomfort.

The more he pushed these thoughts around the less Ridge felt inclined to figure this deal had been set up to catch him with his pants down. Had the client's intention been to find a patsy there'd been no need to go so far afield. Nope. For some special reason someone wanted Cora *dead*.

The outsized bounty, that unusual cash advance left by Benny in this fleabag hotel, had not been conceived for any other reason. So much had been offered because the target was a female, and the job had come to Ridge because he had the rep with Benny of being a man who never failed to deliver.

Ridge had never gunned a woman. But there had to be a first time for just about everything. A bullet didn't care who the hell it got socked into. Only difference made by gender was the hue and cry that was bound to go up. Be louder, more hysterical, and a heap more enduring than the uproar following what had happened to those others. A man would probably better get lost in a hurry. Might be even smarter if a man moved his bankroll south of the border.

Leaving two bits beside his plate Ridge got up, pushed on outside, unwrapped his reins and got into the saddle. The rumble of traffic was already raucous but he sat there a couple of moments wondering if he'd've taken cards in this deal had he known straight off he'd been hired to plunk a woman. He dragged his hand across bristles, guessed it wouldn't have put him off. He'd never lost sleep over none of them others. Price like that she would be snuffed anyway, so why let someone else pick up the kitty?

He hit on a new thought then, a possible angle that hadn't struck him before. If he could manage to discover who had put up that money the stake he was after could be sweetened considerable. He could bleed that sonofabitch for plenty!

He nudged his horse into movement, drifting along through riders and walkers till he came to the Cliff House where he got down again. Looping reins across the peeled pole that was rough with the teethmarks of sundry cribbers, he looked in the lobby and, finding nobody back of the counter, stepped on in and climbed the stairs to stand a couple minutes staring hard at the door behind which he had rendezvoused with Benny. Quietly then he eased it open.

There was a grip on the bed, a rumple of smelly sweat stained shirt, the chipped basin half filled with dirty water. But whoever had belonged to these things wasn't present and Ridge's probing stare found nothing to alarm him. Better leave well enough alone he thought and, backing out, pulled the door shut behind him. Been no indication his cache had been discovered, the dust undisturbed round the feet of that bureau. Why take the risk? he asked himself, scowling. He went back down the stairs, recrossed the empty lobby and was just about to step onto the verandah when the brightness of that screenless doorhold was filled with the shape of an entering man.

Ridge, stepping aside, heard the man's asking voice say, "You staying over?" and found himself faced with Billy Greene again. "Not if I can help it," Ridge answered dryly, and was about to push past when Cora's intended put out a hand. "I had a look at that horse."

Ridge stopped. "What about it?"

"Never saw it before. You in a big hurry?"

"What's on your mind?"

"Been kind of wondering." Greene looked around. "I got a bottle upstairs — you want to come up a minute?"

Ridge shrugged. "All right."

He followed the cowman back up the stairs and into a room several doors down the hall from the one he'd just come from. Greene shut them in, wiped the neck of his bottle and, passing it to Ridge, sat down on the bed. He shoved back his hat. "That business has sure got my mind up."

"If the feller's a stranger he's probably long gone."

"If he was a stranger why bother to cut the brand from that horse? And if he wasn't what's to stop him from trying again? By God, I don't like it!"

"If you're bothered why put it off? Why not marry her right now and get her out of

87

this country? Take her down to that spread you've got —"

"I'd do it quicker than scat if I had the say of it! Happens," Greene said, eyeing Ridge with a scowl, "she's got her heart set on a big Clifton wedding — half the country's been invited."

"When's the happy event comin' off?"

"Sunday a week. Seven days from now. And," he frowned with kind of a snort, "guess who'll be giving the bride away." The boyish face shaped a rueful grin.

"Friend Orren?"

Green nodded disgustedly. "She tell you?"

"No, but it figures. Who's this Judge Turlock?"

"Handled the probate. Old family friend."

"Office here?"

Billy Greene's youthful good looks seemed to dim for a moment as the edge of his glance passed over Ridge's face. "That's right. You won't find him there now, though; he's over to Tucson trying a case. I'd have thought she'd ask *him* to give her away."

"Not if Shackleford had figured to marry her."

"Where'd you get that? First I've heard of it."

"If you'd set up a deal to grab onto Farley's creek wouldn't it appear to seem logical to annex Tadpole, too, while you was at it?"

Billy Greene's eyes narrowed. "You think he's back of what happened to Cora?"

"You don't figure it's in the cards?"

"Why, the man's old enough to . . ." Greene chewed at his lip. "By God it's something to keep in mind. I been doing so dang much thinking about that segundo of hers." Surging up off the bed he took a turn about the room. Stopping by the window he peered unseeingly down at the street. "I don't know . . . far as I've heard that Farley Creek range kind of fell in his lap. Feller that bought Farley out didn't seem able to make a go of it. Way I got it, Spaulding asked Shackleford to put a price on it —"

Greene shrugged. "Could be he did — I'm not that conversant with local history. Maybe Kelly didn't want it or didn't have the cash, or was too short-sighted to realize its worth."

"How come he didn't ask Cora's old man?"

Ridge said after a moment, "If Spaulding was sharp enough to buy Farley out you'd think he'd be spry enough to keep his hold on it. Ever hear what kind of a bind he got into?"

Billy Greene shook his head.

"I heard Orren offered Spaulding a chance to double his money."

Something passed through Greene's stare like doubt. But he offered no comment. Instead, blowing out his breath, he said, "Here's something I picked up when I went out to have me a look at that horse."

Ridge caught the piece of brass that flashed from his hand and, turning it over, looked up to remark, "Cartridge case from a Sharps. Fired recent."

"Ain't that a Sharps I saw on your saddle?"

They looked at each other. "Same caliber," Ridge nodded. "You find this back in the brush?"

"All we've got to find now, it looks like, is somebody packing that kind of rifle."

"Them two shots I fired didn't come from no Sharps."

"Right again," Greene grunted. "I went to the trouble of digging one of your slugs out of that horse." He put the misshapen chunk of lead in Ridge's hand. "Pistol fodder. No doubt about it."

Ridge said, studying Greene's amused glance, "Something's sure settin' heavy on your mind, friend. What is it?"

"According to the sign, when you threw down on that feller you was right by that outcrop. I picked that shell right up out of your tracks."

Ridge stared at the thing, not showing much expression; but deep inside about as taken aback as a man turning up a fifth ace in a poker deck. How could that ranny have known or even *guessed* he was due to be unloaded by anyone packing a weapon as out of date as Ridge's Sharps? Buffalo hunters had favored such a rifle but bison and the killer breed hunting them hadn't been around for years. And how had that jigger known the right caliber to leave where Billy had picked up this brass?

"Pretty slick," he grunted to Greene's watching look. Finally nodding, thinly sighing, he chunked both finds into the pot reposing by the foot of Greene's bed. "Lucky for me you thought to dig out that slug. Could of been a mite embarrassin' if that shell had got picked up by your ambitious friend Cheeko."

"Looks like that feller's out to cook your bacon." When Ridge failed to comment, Billy said, "Must have took that shot at her with the same make and caliber, then slipped back after you'd gone to leave that

91

cartridge case where a unthinking waddy might reckon it pointed at you."

Ridge shrugged.

"Makes him look," Greene said, "to be slicker than slobbers. If we could only talk Cora into staying off her horse a spell, but I don't guess we can . . . not without scaring her silly anyhow. Damn it all — just keeping our eyes peeled don't seem like much force against the style of a feller ingenious as this bird."

"You think of anything better?"

"If I could I'd be doing it, not standing round running off at the mouth," Greene growled through a frown. "You better get back — I think I better move out there myself!"

"Yeah," Ridge nodded. "Not a bad idea. With two of us watchin' we'll have a sight better chance . . . even if it does turn out to be Cheeko."

Greene frowned, the picture of a man fed up with frustrations. "I'll fetch my bronc soon's I pack a few things. See you out front in about twenty minutes. Sooner we get out there better I'll like it."

XI

Though he had not contradicted Greene's assumptions Ridge held certain reservations concerning opinions expressed. He'd recalled the visit paid to his room while he'd been at the livery dickering for that Anchor Bar claybank. While nothing had seemed at the time to be missing, whoever had been through Ridge's belongings had surely seen that taken-apart rifle. He always kept his brass for reloading and, having fetched a few empties along on this trip, was in little doubt where the cartridge case Billy'd picked up had come from.

Was the miserable joker who had pawed through his things Benny's client? Ridge was reasonably sure whoever had done it was the same whippoorwill he'd cut the horse out from under; and that slug chucked at Cora hadn't come from no Sharps!

As he went down the screaky too-steep stairs Ridge found himself thinking of the Paiute Indian who'd got off the stage. He did his best to recollect where the fellow'd got on but it hadn't seemed important enough to stick in his memory. If that redskin was part of this, the toad under the cabbage leaf was a heap more tricky than he'd begun to suspect.

Ridge had no dearth of thoughts to keep him company. Having rubbed against more of life's rough edges than had so far come the way of Cora Lee Kelly he was considerably more curious as to what would have fetched a man with water and 80,000 acres into this isolated region in the first place. Nor was he able to figure what a youngster so happily endowed as handsome Billy Greene could find so enticing in the self-conscious mousy ignoramus he'd apparently set his sights on. Any feller with Greene's all too evident endowments could have had his pick of the litter anyplace.

There just wasn't no accounting for tastes, Ridge reflected. He'd have liked to know, too, which galoot had told Cora he wanted first bid if she ever decided to put the spread on the market. He couldn't see Greene making that kind of offer. Nor was he ready to believe Cheeko Morgan so foolish. Well entrenched as the country's foremost mogul and a friend of the family, Shackleford might have been so bold; it was the only conclusion Ridge could reasonably reach that might explain the girl's reluctance to name him.

He'd have given a pretty for a talk with Judge Turlock. With no chance of that — if he was to put any stock in what Greene had told him — Ridge decided he'd better at the first opportunity take a good look at this Farley Creek setup.

Getting into his saddle another notion struck him and, dismounting again, he stepped back into the lobby to ask the woman straightening things beneath the counter, "Where can I locate Judge Turlock, ma'am?"

"Judge is tryin' a case over to Tucson right now."

"You any idea when he's liable to be back?"

"Land sakes, no! Sooner bet on the antics of a dang jumping bean than try to keep track of *his* comings and goings — Judge's a powerful busy man these days."

Ridge returned to his mount. One thing he could check up he thought, standing there in full smash of the sun, was why Spaulding had got himself shut of Farley's spread. Any number of people ought to be able to tell him that, and if he talked to enough of them he should have the true picture.

He climbed aboard the horse again and rode half a block to the nearest saloon.

The shirt-sleeved man behind the bar wiped a place for him. When he'd drawn Ridge a warm beer and picked up his money, the apron said, "Ed Spaulding?" and chuckled. "Reckon the pressure got too fierce for him."

"What sort of pressure? — here, have one on me."

"Obliged," the man nodded, scooping up Ridge's coin. "Well, if there was any brand he didn't encounter I ain't heard of it. Hard luck sure did camp on Ed's doorstep. A storm came up an' diverted that crick. Skunk fell into his source of drinkin' water. But the thing I guess that finally finished any hopes he had of comin' out on that deal was them nightriders. On top of his cows takin' sick, he went out one mornin' to round up any critters fit to travel an' couldn't turn up more'n a couple dozen steers. Drove 'em over to Anchor Bar that same even' an' asked Orren Shackleford what he'd give for the spread."

"How much *did* he give?"

"If that ever got out it never reached me." The man swabbed at the bar again. "Ed, them days, was pretty chummy with Lafe Murgatroyd. Mebbe he could tell you."

"Where do I find him?"

"Good question. Lafe's a lion hunter.

Got him a boar's nest up in them mountains just north of Anchor Bar. Might have some trouble catchin' him home. Listen for the dogs. That's the best I kin tell you."

Outside on the street with his thoughts tumbling round Ridge peered toward the Cliff House, seeing no sign of Greene. Back in the saddle he elbowed into traffic and rode the wake of a high-wheeled freight rig till he came to the hashhouse he had patronized earlier. He found the mustached proprietor who doubled for cook halfheartedly redding up his pots and pans. To Ridge's query he tugged at his mustache and finally shrugged. "You got me, Jack. Long loopers, I reckon. We've had a plague of 'em around."

"Would you describe Spaulding as a cud-chewin' sort?"

The man rubbed his chin. "Kin o' you'n was he? No? Wal, Ed set out to be long on persistence but some better on hindsight than sizin' things up — though I'm bound to admit he had more troubles than a rat-tailed hoss tied short in fly time. Folks had bets up how long he could take it, an' it looked fer awhile he'd hang on till hell froze an' then strike out acrost the ice. Guess the night them boys paid their final visit was more'n Ed could stand. Fire musta turned his guts to fiddlestrings. He went over nex' day an' sold out to Orren."

"Reckon Shackleford was back of it?"

"You ain't goin' to hear me say so."

Billy Greene was waiting when Ridge reached the hotel. "You been eating again?" Ridge shook his head. Greene said as he climbed into his hull, "I'm going to be about as popular with that one-eyed segundo as a polecat at a box social."

Ridge said, "You'll damn sure have company." Greene looked at him, puzzled, but Ridge couldn't see much point in explaining. Each busy with his thoughts, conversation lagged. It was two hours past supper when they came off the spur to sit looking down into Tadpole's yard.

"What do I tell Cora?" grumbled Billy, twisting his head around.

"Don't look at me. It was your idea."

"Yeah. Seemed smarter back in town. I don't want nothing to happen to that girl, but . . ."

"Tell her that, then. Don't you find that truth in the long run is best?"

"It's a cinch you ain't been much around women!" Still frowning, Greene put his horse in motion. When they came into the yard Ridge offered, sober faced: "You don't have to move right into the house with her."

Billy said, disgusted, "Thanks a lot," and got out of his saddle in front of two hands hunkered on boot heels alongside the bunkhouse disinterestedly watching a tobacco-cudded third laconically reducing a length of stick into shavings. "Morgan round?"

"Nope," the tobacco chewer said after spitting. The other two speculatively peered up at Ridge.

"Reckon," Billy said, "he's probably over talking to Cora," and, dropping his reins, struck out for the house. Ridge, still in the saddle, got out the makings and twisted up a smoke. He was just putting fire to it when Greene with an unsettled look came striding up to demand: "Where's Miss Kelly?"

The whittler, looking him over, resettled his chew to presently observe, "We ain't what you might call in her confidence."

A flush came into Greene's boyish face. The eyes held a shine above his tightening jaw and even though it was almost dark a man could see the temper working in him.

Ridge's quiet drawl asked, "Anybody know where Morgan's at?"

"Reckon he's gone to hev a talk with that lion hunter."

"Murgatroyd?"

"He's the on'y one round got the right kinda dogs."

"What's dogs got to do with it?"

The men swapped looks. In a tone just bordering the edge of sarcasm the whittler said, "He don't figure to hunt that cat by himself." One of the others spoke up. "Found two chewed-up calfs south of Turkey. Three more las' week."

"How long's he been gone?"

"Mebbe Coosie can say. He'd left 'fore we got in."

Ridge, Greene trailing, rode across to the cook shack. The dour faced dough wrangler got in first lick. "Next meal's breakfast. Come back at four thirty."

Ridge said crisply: "Where-at's Cora Lee?"

"Miz Kelly you mean?"

"You hear pretty good."

"Took her horse fer a gallop."

Greene cut in, impatient, "What time was this?"

"Shank of the evenin'. Round about three I'd say at a guess."

"Before," Ridge said, "or after Morgan pulled out?"

"After. Just after."

XII

Away from the cook shack Ridge said as Greene, fisting the reins with a handful of hair, swung aboard his horse, "Looks like some of that talk about Cheeko rubbed off after all."

"Want to chew that a little finer?"

"Them suspicions you been airin' appears to of fell on fertile ground." To the cowman's blank gaze: "Don't it ring no bells she took off after him?"

Greene's narrowing stare beat against Ridge's face. "You trying to say she set out to *follow* him?"

"That's the general idea."

"Jesus Christ!" Greene exclaimed. "What are we waitin' on?"

He yanked the head of his horse around, stopped short when he saw Ridge, motionless, watching. "Well?"

"You goin' off half cocked?"

"I'm going to roust out the crew!"

"You better try usin' your head for a change." Greene's affronted stare began to glint with resentment. Ridge said, unperturbed: "How far do you figure these ponies will take us?" And while the younger man was turning that over, "You give any thought to whose crew this is?"

"Cora's paying their wages —"

"That don't cut any ice. If your notions about Cheeko come anywhere near the straight of it the most of these boys'll stay right where they're at." He watched Greene digest this.

With an obvious attempt to curb his impatience Greene said darkly, "I ain't forgot a horse took her old man over a cliff. I don't want to find her down in some gulch!"

"If Morgan had any part in that he'd have to be ready for a string of spools to imagine he could pull that kind of thing again."

"He could find some other way of serving his purpose."

"So we'll rope out fresh horses and take a pasear off into the blue, and when we've made sure no one's keepin' cases we'll kind of drift in the direction of that lion hunter's shack. That make sense to you?"

Greene fidgeted some but, unable to come up with anything better, wheeled his mount and set off for the day pen. Ridge forefooted his Anchor Bar claybank while Greene dropped his loop around the neck

102

of a snorting black which he saddled and mounted, sitting in disgusted impatience as he waited for Ridge to fetch his Sharps from the bunkhouse.

"What did that fool of a Windy want?"

"Wanted to know," Ridge chuckled, "if we figured to go huntin' that cat in the dark. Said I guessed if Morgan could we might as well take a whack at it, too."

"You think they'll stay put?"

"We'll likely find out before we're much older."

Ridge pulled up after they'd gone half a mile. "We'll wait ten minutes back of that jag of squattin' cedars."

Sitting their mounts inside the thicket, time took on an extra dimension. Far as Ridge was concerned this jaunt was a snipe hunt, but he could see plain enough how Greene must feel. And to do the kid justice it was possible, of course, his suspicions of Cora's segundo just might turn out to have some foundation — not that Ridge, in his own mind, doubted Morgan's bent.

Number One would have come first with Cheeko every time. But the man would have to be a jibbering idjot to try any underhanded tricks tonight.

An orange moon began to show its face above the black sprawl of distant rim rocks as Ridge said irritably, "Can't you keep that damned hide's head still?" though he knew well enough the fidgeting horse was only reflecting its rider's impatience.

When three or four more minutes dragged themselves past without any sign or sound of activity he growled: "Let's get on with it — if they'd been coming they'd be out here by now."

The brief wait had at any rate increased visibility, though not to the extent of un-covering any tracks. They had very little choice when it came to direction, the nat-ural lay of the land easily defining the most likely course between Tadpole and those shimmering escarpments north of Anchor Bar. No girl was going to elect to climb mountains when a smoother way lay right in front of her — without, of course, Cheeko'd gone someplace which had nothing to do with dogs or lions.

Ridge presently said, "We on Shackleford's range?"

"Past quarter-hour — the Farley Creek strip."

"Where's the water you wanted?"

"We'll be crossing it directly. About an-other half mile. Runs through that line of brush off there."

While reasonably certain the Tadpole

segundo hadn't anything in mind immediately likely to jeopardize the girl's health *(even if the fellow had taken that shot at her)*, Ridge — with Billy so stirred up about it — found himself darkly wondering when he would encounter another situation as favorably inclined toward a successful culmination of his contract. She might never again be so prone as right now, away from the ranch and alone in the night on the probable route taken by a man Greene would swear had it in for her.

He tugged the hat more firmly across a bleak stare. "Got the time on you, Billy?"

Greene dug out his watch, held it squinting before his face. Unable to read it, with a disgusted grumble he dragged the head of a match across the hip of his Levi's. As it burst into flame another light winked and he dropped the stick in a wild grab for leather as the screech of a bullet was drowned by the sudden sharp crack of a rifle.

With both mounts up on their hind legs, snorting, other lights winked from that dark line of brush and a huddle of horsebackers bulged into sight yipping like coyotes.

Apparently not anxious to become a dead hero Greene spun his horse and kicked it into a run without even pausing to throw a glance in Ridge's direction.

Being able to tell skunks from housecats without recourse to any crystal ball Ridge wasn't doing much loitering either, and a split second later put the steel to his claybank to go barreling off in another direction designed — if this didn't break up pursuit — to at least minimize the likelihood of having his mount shot from under him.

Ten minutes later when he pulled up to listen there wasn't any sounds being thrown up behind him. He guessed those nightriding sons had either given up the chase or gone skally-hootin' off after Billy Greene.

Kind of made a man feel like believing in Santa!

While not a few leather slappers in his line of business had found their way into unmarked graves Ridge Butler — though not lately active — was still on the hoof because, besides being eminently practical, he seldom drank anything stronger than beer, kept himself to himself and, working or idle, stayed clear of crowds and was eternally vigilant.

It was this constant habit of sizing things up to the last deadly decimal that swung his thoughts now to the unfinished chore which had fetched him into this mountainous country. Somewhere in this wild sweep of range Cora Lee Kelly was riding, either alone or with Cheeko Morgan. Experience told him, as well as plain horse sense, he might not again encounter half as good a chance. Night riders rampant; Morgan on the loose someplace in her vicinity — about as likely a setup as he could hope to run into.

He rubbed the back of a hand against bristled chin while he studied the night and the look of things round him, considering the best way of coming up with her.

With the head start he'd had Cheeko, by now — if he'd gone straight to Murgatroyd's and found the man home — should be on his way back. Ridge didn't reckon the dogs would be with him, or the lion hunter either. And, if Cora hadn't lost Cheeko or been discovered by him, she ought still to be somewhere in his wake, bound home also. Back three or four miles in that narrow canyon he'd come through with Greene looked the best place a man could meet up with them. They'd almost have to pass through it unless Morgan had other chores on his mind.

Which he might if Greene were right and it turned out to be Cora's segundo after all that was sardonically shuffling the cards in his deal. And wasn't it, by God, just a smidgin odd they should have jumped those cattle thieves along the same trail presumably taken by Morgan? Was Cheeko their boss and this how he'd piled up them dollars for Benny?

With a picture of Morgan's scowling, ferociously staring black-patched face before his mind's eye, Ridge could hardly help wondering if Cheeko'd been with them — maybe fired that first shot. Perhaps, Ridge reflected, he might earlier have grabbed the wrong end of the iron in imagining her range boss tonight, of all times, couldn't afford to have anything happen to Cora. If she'd seen him with those nightriding rannies he could hardly afford . . .

With an irascible grunt Ridge was about to wheel his mount toward that canyon when a distant mutter of hoofs fetched his head up, locking him, listening, into his tracks.

XIII

Quietly Ridge lifted the gun from its perch on his hip.

Much clearer now come the sound of hooves drifting down off some high place. Just the one set, sometimes fainter, abruptly loudening, carried steadily nearer on the trickle of breeze he felt curling around him. Greene, was it? Cheeko? One of that bunch who'd roared out of the brush? Or someone who had no concern with this business?

The night was alive with the brassy taste of danger while Ridge, head canted, waited motionless and ready for whatever might emerge from the shrouded blue-black yonder. A thin damp fog lay along the ground, dappled with silver where moon's light touched the revolving convolutions that were scurrying, wind-harried, in lacelike wisps and stringers across the thorny growth. Ridge's horse blew out a gusty breath and on that instant all sound ceased.

Times like this Ridge had the patience of an Apache. Pistol up, finger on trigger, he sat ready to fire at the first sign of flight.

Something struck and bounced in the nearby shale and he silently grinned from his seat in the saddle till it crossed his mind a man near enough to chunk a cartridge that close ought to be in plain sight!

Watchful, edgy, with considerable care he twisted his head first left and then right without latching onto the faintest impression of the cartridge tosser's placement. Bending forward to limn the gelding's head against mist that he might see the cocked ears, he bent a little more and glimpsed, where they pointed, a vague blotch in the shadows. But this shift of weight made the saddle screak and a jumpety voice cried out: *"Who is it?"*

Who but Cora would have bothered to ask!

Sweat from his finger lay cold on the trigger. Face to face with the chance he'd been hunting, with the fool girl right there under his gun, Ridge bitterly furious heard himself mutter, "That you, Kelly?"

He ought by God to be bored for the samples!

"Ridge?" she called, coming toward him. "Gosh! You gave me a turn!" She didn't have to underscore it; her relief was evident.

"Your friend Billy's fit to be tied," Ridge grumbled, stuffing his shooter back into leather. "He's out hunting you now. Thought if I wasn't handy you agreed to stay put —"

"I know. But when Morgan saddled up and took off in the direction of Anchor Bar all Billy's talk suddenly seemed to make sense. You weren't around and . . . anyway I decided to follow him —"

Ridge said harshly: "You could have got yourself killed!"

"Well, I didn't. And Morgan didn't go to Orren's after all."

"Probably discovered you was camped on his shirttail."

"I don't see how. No Indian could have been more careful. I never got nearer than a good half mile of him and wherever it was open I got up on a hill and watched till he went into the roughs again."

She swung in beside him as Ridge turned the claybank toward Tadpole headquarters. "I'm glad I went. I'm satisfied now Billy's suspicions are preposterous — there just isn't anything to be suspicious about! If Morgan had gone to Anchor Bar after all he's said to me about Orren . . . but he didn't. He went to see a lion hunter about that cat that's been killing our calfs."

"You know that?"

"Of course I know. I fetched Dad's Army glass and watched the two of them discuss —"

"They could've been talkin' about something else."

"Well, they weren't. I waited till I saw Lafe get out his dogs. Billy's wrong. There just isn't any basis for thinking Cheeko Morgan is teamed up with Orren to get this ranch away from me. It's about as silly as thinking Orren Shackleford with all he's got could possibly be scheming —"

"All he's got he sure wasn't born with," Ridge pointed out, "nor he didn't get his hooks on that much range by goin' to church reg'lar and settin' there pious while it fell into his lap like that manna they talk about."

"The man is my godfather!" Cora said shortly, like being in that position wasn't no different than being equipped with wings, harp and halo; and Ridge subsided into smoldering thoughts.

It wasn't too late yet to fashion some kind of accident, he reckoned, but with that bunch of nightriders wheeling their horses through his cogitations his head was too filled to give proper mind to it. He still had six days to get down to cases according to the program as laid down by Benny. He couldn't really see what the hell the big rush was, except six days hence was the date Cora'd set for putting on double harness.

He was up next morning in time to eat with the crew. Morgan was there in his place at the head of the table, eating with his hat on, unapproachably wrapped in a caustic silence, the one tawny, glowering, uncovered eye unforgettably ugly as galvanized sin. Glance caught again by the stone home-fashioned bola holding hat straps together beneath the segundo's cold-jawed chin, Ridge asked as the range boss, finishing, shoved back his chair, "Greene take off?"

Despite the evidence of enmity so obviously enveloping him Morgan paused to peer with what may have been a jab of startled surprise. Gone too swift to be properly read, with his face wiped clean Cheeko grunted, "Ain't seen him," and went on outside, the rest of the crew getting up to tramp after him.

"You see him, Coosie?"

Cook shook his head, began picking up emptied cups and plates which he packed, with the eating tools, the length of the room and sloshed disgustedly into the wreck pan.

"Didn't he come in last night?"

"I got enough to do without keepin' tabs on comin's an' goin's that ain't none of my never-mind," the pot wrangler gruffed. "You goin' to set there all day?" he irascibly asked.

On the stoop Ridge paused to scowl toward the house but, not in a mood to swap gab with the girl, bent his steps toward where the outfit was roping out mounts, cheeks still creased in the traces of a frown. Partway there he pulled up and swung round to drag spurs across the yard and poke his head in the bunkhouse door. Green's gear still lay on a stripped-bare bunk.

With stare turned thoughtful Ridge put together a smoke. He went back to the cook shack without bothering to fire up but, realizing he'd get no change out of Coosie, hunkered by the doorstep till the crew rode off. Then flinging down the unlit quirly he put his hull on the claybank and struck out toward Shackleford's over the same ground he'd traveled last night with Billy Greene.

He wasted no time hunting for tracks but rode with both eyes peeled, having no idea where Cheeko was now and no intention of being taken unawares. Several times in the first half hour he caught distant glimpses of one or another of the Tadpole crew going about the chores laid out for them, but saw no sign of Morgan's chin-strapped sombrero.

When he judged he'd got into the Farley Creek area he began looking round with considerably more interest. Grass here looked better, not noticeably longer but there was more of it and the color was stronger. Most of what few cows he encountered carried Shackleford's mark and appeared in prime condition.

He was mildly astonished from what he'd heard about this situation not to have run into any Anchor Bar hands. Since he'd encountered no fences he found it difficult to understand, if Cora's friend Orren wasn't patrolling this feed, why other folks' cattle hadn't helped themselves to it.

It came into Ridge's head when he sighted the brush outlining the course of Farley's creek that, instead of nightriders hunting free beef, the bunch which had jumped Greene and him might well have been some of Shackleford's punchers. The more he pushed this around the more likely it seemed. Yet — if this were so and they'd come up with him — where was Greene now? Had Billy connected with one of those slugs before that bunch had learned who they were shooting at?

Ridge started cutting for sign, finding more than enough, but in such confused jumble the tracks added little to his grasp of what had happened. He dragged a hand down across the feel of smooth cheeks and frowningly peered through the windless shimmer of midday heat at the hogbacks and hummocks of half-buried mesquites. A visit to Anchor Bar might prove more enlightening than chasing on through another couple hours of this glare in the thin hope of learning something definite from the torn-up ground left from last night's encounter. Still, if that bunch had not been part of Orren's crew Greene might be lying bad hurt out there someplace.

It was this that decided him against better judgment.

XIV

It was no trouble following the tracks beaten into the rain by that wild chase. What kept nagging at Ridge's mind was the ferocious determination with which that whole bunch had gone pounding after Greene. It seemed almost as though they must have recognized Billy, and this was the thought which most baffled him now. He couldn't make any kind of sense from this unless indeed those men were part of Shackleford's crew and the Anchor Bar owner, for some dark reason, meant to put Cora's intended where no amount of sun would ever make him sweat again.

It was well past noon and Ridge was deep in a tangle of steepening hills when he came to where the pursuit had pulled up. Far as he could determine they'd milled around in this locality for a considerable while before regrouping to go straggling off into a southerly direction; and there was no indication from the trampled ground whether they'd gotten the job done or plain given up.

Another quarter-hour of meticulous

searching failed to turn up any single set of tracks which might have been made by an escaping Billy Greene. Was the man buried here or bound for the same end someplace else?

Higher up over there, well above Ridge's stance, shaggy junipers made a green huddle against the sheer rock of those red cliffs above and, eyeing that slope, he tried to imagine how this would have looked in the dark. There'd been a moon last night but a man, if he could have managed to get up there, might just possibly have got clean away.

On this thin chance Ridge quit his horse. There was nothing to show Greene had made this trek; but afoot, with nothing in the scrub and shale to indicate where he's set out from, it wasn't too likely Billy'd left much sign.

It proved a pretty stiff climb, taking more time and wind than he had thought to give. When he finally got into the junipers Ridge swore. The ground up here, while limber enough, held no evidence of anyone's passage.

Ridge stood a while scowling, catching up with his breath, before he began the risky trip down to where his gelding was munching on bushes. Back in the saddle

118

Ridge peered round before again taking up the trail left by Greene's pursuers.

By all the sign and signal smokes this crew was traveling head-on toward Tadpole and he was damned if he could figure that, either. That he might be dealing with chin-strapped Cheeko appeared straightaway to look more than likely; but without Greene was dead it didn't make sense Cora's segundo would fetch him back to the ranch regardless of how smooth a story they'd hatched.

Woolling this round, the next three or four miles failed to disclose any plausible answers; and then, abruptly, the horse-backers — still half the distance short of Tadpole headquarters — swung back into the east and ten minutes later dragged another herring sharp across their tracks. That suddenly the bunch — all five of them — broke up and took off singly in as many directions.

Scowling disgustedly, Ridge took the trouble to painstakingly scrutinize each set of hoofprints, find nothing significant beyond the impression none of these horses had been packing double. So where had Greene got to? *Was he forking one of them?*

Shackleford hoisted his sawed-off shape

off a hide-bottomed rocker as Ridge pulled up twenty feet from the porch at Anchor Bar headquarters. His smiling countenance ignored the grim set of Butler's jaw to call out in that astonishingly deep voice. "Get down and set a spell. How's things at Tadpole? What's Cora Lee got up her sleeve now?"

"I ain't had time to look this mornin'." Still in the saddle Ridge said shortly: "Your crew all accounted for?"

"Far as I know."

"Lose any stock last night?"

Head to one side Anchor Bar's owner looked Ridge over with a closer attention. "What's this all about?"

"You haven't answered the question."

Orren Shackleford snorted. "If we have it's the first I've heard about it. You ride clean over here to ask me that?"

"How do you feel about this feller Greene?"

"How do *you* feel about him?" Shackleford countered and, when this got no change, said, "I think Cora's making a considerable mistake."

"You tell her that?"

"Hardly." The cowman said dryly, "Speaking of women, I found out long ago you tell 'em what they want to hear or keep your damnfool mouth shut."

"So what have you got against Greene?"

Shackleford tapped out his pipe on the porch rail and, still watching Ridge, stuffed it into his pocket. "Kind of lightweight, isn't he?"

"Right now he's missin'," Ridge said bluntly. "Ain't shown much use for Cora's segundo and been pretty frank about telling her so — seems to believe Morgan's got his sights set on takin' over that property. Some of his talk must've rubbed off on her. Shank of the evenin' yesterday Cheeko set out someplace all by himself. Cora piled on a hull an' took off after him."

"That was a rattlebrained thing to do — but that's Cora, all right. Leap first and think later."

"Yeah. Well, Greene had come out from town and the pair of us caught up fresh ponies and went lookin'. They been losing some young stuff; seems Cheeko told Coosie he was goin' after that lion man, Murgatroyd. It was dark when we left Tadpole — no change of readin' sign. We run into an ambush at Farley's creek. We split up with them fellers burnin' powder like it was going out of fashion.

"Seems the whole push concentrated on

Greene." Briefly Ridge filled Shackleford in. "Wasn't a sign of him I could find where that bunch milled around up there in the roughs. They was pointed again towards that creek when the tracks split up and I come on over here."

Shackleford stood a while turning it over. "Think Greene was with them?"

"I dunno what to think."

The cowman said more sharply, "You don't figure he's *dead,* do you?"

"Unless he got clean away somehow, I sure can't see any other . . ."

The old man sighed. "She's like to take this hard." There was concern in his face. "You want me to go over there and talk to her?"

Ridge sighed, too, blowing out his breath in a snarl of frustration. "Don't suppose, do you, they . . . that doesn't make sense! I was thinkin' the idea, maybe, was to keep him out of sight and make it look at that weddin' like he'd run out on her — left her waitin' at the altar."

Shackleford said to Ridge's searching stare, "You reckon Morgan would figure she'd turn to him then?"

"Won't wash. Wasn't none of them rannies packin' double."

"You can't be sure," the ranch owner

said. "Not just from looking at a passel of tracks." When Ridge shrugged the old man muttered with his glance winging round, "You find his horse?"

Ridge shook his head.

"How much looking did you do up there?"

"Plenty."

"Well, it could have gone back to the ranch if it was loose."

"His horse hadn't come in when I set out this mornin'."

Shackleford scratched at his jaw. "So maybe he rode off with those boys. On his own horse. You thought about that?"

"Five ponies went up there chasin' Greene. Five ponies come back an' split up not three miles from here. If Billy's mount was one of 'em *and he was on it,* what happened to the sixth horse and man that went up there?"

Shackleford said with an edge to his tone, "That ain't the part that sticks in my craw. I've got a sneaky damn feeling some two-legged polecat's setting me up to catch a rap out of this!"

The frosty glint of his stare grabbed at Ridge, and soft as a goosehair pillow he said, "You make this look like any doing of mine you better start leaving wide-apart tracks."

XV

Riding into the evening heel of the sun on his way back to Tadpole, Ridge with so much slogging through his head could not make up his mind which of that pair had been the real Shackleford — the hearty Orren who'd fetched out the welcome mat or the livid-faced one he had looked at last.

They could both be real when you got right down to it.

Any mogul might show the knot in his tail if forced to stand on his stoop hearing some hired saddle stiff running off at the mouth to all but accuse him of engineering something he'd had nothing to do with.

The set of tracks Ridge had followed and finally lost within scarcely a stone's throw of Anchor Bar headquarters could have been left by anyone; it didn't have to be Orren or some galoot on his payroll. The tracks could have been put there, this whole play masterminded, by Benny's client. The one who wanted to get rid of Cora.

Ridge hadn't glimpsed or heard anything yet which convinced him the name of that person was Shackleford. While it did seem 'friend' Orren might appear the most likely, no search of the facts could figure how Cora's removal was like to advantage him.

Greene's disappearance was a different kettle of fish.

By getting rid of the man she was betrothed to, Orren — if his goal was acquirement of Tadpole — would have opened the way to any number of interesting possibilities. This same set of circumstances looked just as good with Cheeko Morgan as the man who pulled the strings. About the only one this situation was not built to benefit was the apparent object of all that maneuvering — Greene himself.

Perhaps, Ridge reflected, he was reading too much into whatever fate had caught up with Billy. On the face of things that bunch could be just what he and Greene had assumed, nightriders jumped while trying to lift someone's cattle. With their edge in numbers what more natural than to show fight?

Which was all very well, he scowlingly decided, but why would the whole push have gone after Greene? This was something he found hard to swallow. And it came into his mind like a gust of cold wind that these speculations and the energy expended was about as futile as attempting to scratch one's head with one's elbow, in no way advancing the purpose which had brought him into this country.

It was full dark when the plodding hoofs of Ridge's Anchor Bar claybank fetched him into the lanes of butter-yellow light spilling from the windows across Tadpole's yard.

He did not notice anything out of the ordinary but his habitual care passed a glance through the shadows, sifting each one, as he kneed the gelding toward the corrals. Stepping out of the saddle he pulled off his gear, rubbed the horse down and slapped him into the day pen. Then he put up the bars and went to fork him some hay. He had just reached the stack when a shape materialized out of the blackness shrouding the open-fronted shed where saddle strings were shod. Flash of green stone beneath the man's chin would have told Ridge even if the sombrero hadn't it was Morgan coming toward him. "Want a word with you," Morgan gruffed.

Ridge waited, silent.

"Wanta know what the hell's goin' on around here. Where's Greene?"

"Good question."

Cheeko scowled. "Didn't he ride out from town with you las' night?"

"That's right."

"An' after jawin' with Coosie didn't the pair of you rope fresh mounts an' ride off?"

Ridge nodded.

Morgan said abruptly, "What'd you want t' see me about?"

"It was Cora we was looking for. Run into some rifles at Farley's creek and, duckin' blue whistlers, lost track of each other. I haven't seen hide nor hair of Greene since."

This apparently was news to Cheeko, but just which part of it was not at once obvious. After some moments, "Went huntin' him, didn't you?" the range boss grumbled.

"That's right. After I found out this morning he hadn't come in." With several courses in view Ridge went on to go over what he'd found out, winding up with his visit to Anchor Bar and the manner in which he and Orren had parted.

"Shackleford's lyin'," the segundo snapped. "That bunch come from Anchor Bar!"

"If you've proof —"

Cheeko made a rude noise. "That son of a bitch puts on more dog than a Mex'kin officer of revenue! Got all the mealymouths lickin' his boots but he don't fool me, by God, fer a minute! Farley seen through him — that's why he sold out. Knew he'd no more chance than a broke-leg grasshopper afoot in a ant hill! Ed Spaulding had guts but couldn't cut it, either. If he'd've stuck with it one more night he'd been out there stretchin' hemp someplace with a card pinned on him warnin' off rustlers!"

Ridge shrugged. "That's pretty strong talk, but unless you've got proof, the kind that'll stand up in front of a jury —"

"You'll git no jury round here t' convict him! He's got this range in a forked stick, mister." With a final hard stare he made as though to stomp off, then turned with a glower to growl over his shoulder, "Girl know about this?"

"I haven't been over there."

Morgan chewed at his cheek. "Prob'ly roust out the whole outfit t' hunt him." Then said with a shake of the head, "Sets a heap of store by that peckerneck dude."

Watching the man stride away, Ridge wondered how much of that talk you could bank on. Fellow had first of all to take into account the galling emotions smoldering inside Cora's range boss as a result of the humiliation suffered at Ridge's hands. That he'd managed to keep his rage pretty well banked was some indication of the man's scope and character. Why, if he felt so lathered about Shackleford, had he been so determined not to have Ridge around? It almost had to go deeper than just Cora's hiring Ridge over his head. Had he really imagined Ridge was in Orren's pay? Or had he had some deeper, more personal reason for wanting no strangers around this place? Despite what the man had just now said, Ridge — recalling Greene's arrival that first night here — was reminded Cheeko's reaction to Billy had not been hidden underneath any woodpile.

Ridge took the hay to his nickering horse, then went across to the barn and fetched a measure of oats, still thinking about the Tadpole segundo. He took a look in the trough to make sure there was water and with another glance round, crossed the yard to the house. Stepping onto the gallery he put a fist to the door. Despite the lamp in the front room's window he had quite a wait before the girl came to peer through the sagging screen.

"Ridge Butler," he said. "Mind if I come in?"

She pushed open the door but did not ask him to sit. He thought in the lamp's light she seemed a little flushed. Like maybe she'd been crying, though he had not reckoned her the crying kind.

"What is it?" she asked. "Have you come about Billy?"

"Yeah. I didn't find him."

When she kept watching him, not speaking, Ridge told of the day, giving an account of his travels and the gist of his conversation with Shackleford. "But the fact is," he finished, "regardless of anything else, the one set of tracks that took me to Anchor Bar I followed to within walking distance of the house."

The girl chewed her lip. "I'm not surprised he was riled if that's how you put it when you talked to Orren. You might as well have said that bunch was part of his crew."

"For all I know they were," Ridge growled. "That one feller —"

"That's just it. You said they broke up, that the tracks you followed took you to Orren's. Who's to say each of the other four didn't lay a trail to four other outfits? It's at least as reasonable as what you implied." She stared at him as though expecting an argument. When she didn't get it, she asked rather sharply, "Didn't you think it odd after coming so far the tracks suddenly vanished just short of Orren's doorstep?"

"Not much. They'd been worked over with a greasewood switch. Whoever elected to rub them out must of been in a hurry and got a mite careless." Ridge said with curled lip, "Between where them tracks quit and Shackleford's handiest buildin' this peckerneck overlooked a couple of prints. The horse is at Anchor Bar. Galoot who rubbed out that trail is there too, or damn sure has *been* there."

The room got quiet as an empty cup. No flush was staining Cora's cheeks now. Bone-white was the face behind that green stare of wide-sprung angry frightened eyes.

Ridge said brutally: "Which is it you're really worried about, Greene or friend Orren?"

Before she could answer an affronted voice cried, "I won't have you bullying Cora like that!" and a tight faced Greene appeared suddenly behind her.

XVI

"Well," Ridge said. And "Well!" again.

There was a greasy shine to Billy's face where light from the coal-oil lamp struck across it as the girl stepped back to peer, flushed again, from one to the other.

Greene licked dry lips. "It's not like you think —"

"I was readin' sign while you was still wrapped in three-cornered pants!"

"That's not what I meant," Cora's man said too loud, then ruefully smiled like a kid with pockets stuffed full of apples.

Ridge's stare went over the bench-made boots. "Was it you left them tracks in Shackleford's yard?"

Billy took a fresh breath. "I'm not that good."

"Any galoot who can get home free from the kind of bind them fellers had *you* in is pretty damn good in any gent's language."

Greene with distress on his collar-ad face declared, "Had me a bit of luck is all — extraordinary, really. Remember that pine just before you got into that drop where they lost me? That and the moon is what saved my bacon. Looking back, never guessing that bunch had been driving me into a box, I was appalled to realize they were almost onto me. I caught a glimpse of the pine and that low hanging branch stretched out over the rail and, just about then, the moon went behind clouds."

Greene shook his head. "You'll find this hard to believe. I made a wild leap and got onto that branch and not two seconds later they roared past beneath me. That's all there was to it. Nothing clever about it. Just bullheaded luck."

"Don't suppose," Ridge said, "they ever looked at that tree. But what happened to your nag? How come they didn't find it?"

"He never went down there. When I quit the saddle he left the trail."

Ridge looked at him straightly. "Guess we don't have to do no more guessin'. You ought to be able to put names to all of 'em. All that time you spent up in that tree?"

"But I didn't," Billy said with a nervous grin. "Soon's they went past I dropped down out of there. Went after my horse, but that was far as my luck carried me. I never did find him."

"How'd you get back?"

"Shanks' mare." Greene sighed. "Spent the whole night walking — just got here in fact. Stayed hid out in the brush all day. Had no way of knowing they had given up on me."

Ridge eyed him out of a wooden face. "Then you've no idea who those hombres were or why they were in such a sweat to come up with you?"

Greene shook his head, looking honestly baffled.

"Cheeko know you're back?"

"Not from me he don't."

Cora Lee said, "Billy thinks Morgan would like nothing better than to see him packed up behind six black horses. It's purely ridiculous, but he's convinced himself Cheeko means to get hold of this ranch by fair means or foul."

"If he believes that why hasn't he faced Morgan with it?" Ridge said to the man, "You're not afraid of him are you?"

Greene growled, reddening, "Cora won't hear to it. If I had my way . . ." He flung out his hands with a frustrated look. "It's the only thing we argue about. If she'd let me I'd send him packing in a minute!"

The girl gave a nervous little bark of a laugh. With her face coming round she told Ridge defensively, "He knows his job. He does his work — he's always been loyal to our best interests. If my father could trust him there's no reason I shouldn't."

Greene said grimly, "A horse took your father over a cliff."

"A horse," she nodded, "not Cheeko Morgan."

"I wouldn't bet he'd nothing to do with it!"

"You see?" Cora Lee said to Ridge, tartly smiling.

Ridge had no interest in their private frictions nor any intention of being drawn into them. Pulling his glance from the girl he asked, "You got any plans for the immediate future? I mean, what do you figure to do about this?"

"What *can* I do? I don't know who's involved, even."

Ridge could have told them what Morgan thought, that Shackleford was back of whatever happened in this locality; but fed up with talk he said somewhat gruffly, "You goin' to keep out of sight till it's time for that splicing?"

A gusty breath fell out of Greene, but he had enough hold on the strings of his temper to smother whatever resentment he felt. Bringing up his chin with that boyish grin, "Guess I'll just rock along for a while," he said coolly. If he had any plans, he wasn't spreading them around for a hired gun to shoot at.

Outside on the gallery Ridge stood a moment considering the tug of things left undone, shoving them back of more urgent necessities, seeking out the shape of the barracks-like bunkhouse, both eyes peeled as he crossed the dark yard.

Inside it was clear, by the snoring, that the crew was sacked out; but Morgan's bunk was empty when he passed it. Scooping up his blankets Ridge went back to the day pen, pausing some seconds to have a hard look around. With saddle and Sharps, bone tired, he followed the poles to the pen's darker side where he spread out his bed and, pulling off only his hat, got into it.

Greene's account of his escape could be essentially true, yet a man would be a fool to take the fellow at his own valuation. Nor was Ridge buying Cora's notion. Cow stealers rather tended to keep things simple; though of course if Cheeko had the right of it, Orren was the impetus behind these nightriders, he would hardly care to have them bedded down at Anchor Bar.

Whether that bunch were rustlers or not Shackleford *could* be back of them. So could Cheeko. It wouldn't be the first time a cattle king or unscrupulous range boss had put on a different hat in the dark and attempted to shortcut a hidden bent.

There was certainly a chance the whole idea behind that moonlit pursuit of Greene had been aimed at turning out Tadpole to hunt him. From what Ridge had seen of him Shackleford was smart.

Tired though he was Ridge couldn't get to sleep. And the more he searched churning thoughts for some acceptable answer the more inclined he felt to cut his string and drop the whole mess. The longer he stayed the greater the risks. He was like a fifth wheel that nobody wanted. Save maybe the girl he had come here to kill.

Even Cora, though she'd hired him, appeared to be having second thoughts. He'd less than five days now to fulfill his contract. Be a whole heap more sensible to cut his losses, take what Benny'd given him and haul his freight.

Every instinct, all his experience, warned him to drop this deal and get out. He could be across the border and deep into Mexico before Flores and his client discovered he'd run out on them. And tomorrow, by God, he might do just that!

★ ★ ★

The night passed without any untoward alarms, but mood and outlook were not much improved when the impatient prod of a rib-jolting boot fetched him out of the clutch of feverish dreams to find the sun well up and Cora Lee Kelly disgustedly eyeing him.

"Some watchdog you are!" she exclaimed, plainly vexed.

Not bothering to answer he got himself up and, grunting, ducked between rails to splash his face with water from the trough, ignoring the whinnyings of his hungry horse.

When he felt more up to facing another day's frustrations he climbed back out and clapped on his hat. He was bending to gather up his gear when Cora said in a low, guarded voice hardly more than a whisper: "I want you to ride into Clifton for me. Straightaway."

Ridge peered irritably. "It was protection you hired, not a errand boy."

A deepening color spread through her cheeks. He watched jaws clench, hazel eyes fill with anger. "You were hired to do whatever I say do."

"Not me," Ridge growled. "I'm nobody's lackey." He looked at her bleakly. "You got

138

plenty of hands. Send Cheeko. Or Billy —"

"Billy's already left. So has Morgan, for that matter." She said more reasonably, "There's nobody round here now but Coosie. If you won't go I'll have to ride in myself."

"Where'd Billy go?"

"He was gone when I got up."

Ridge heaved his saddle to the pen's top rail. He got out the Sharps from under his blankets. "What's so important you want to send me to town for?"

"I want you to fetch Judge Turlock out here."

"Heard the Judge was in Tucson."

"He's in Clifton now. He told me before he left he'd be back on the twelfth — in plenty of time for the wedding," she said to Ridge's stare.

"And you've no idea where Billy is now?"

The girl's eyes looked at Ridge unreadably. "No. Billy," she said with every evidence of care, "is subject to sudden . . . enthusiasms. Sometimes I don't think he will ever grow up."

That was one way of putting it, Ridge reckoned, frowning. Likely part of his charm, far as women were concerned — appealed to the mother in them. Just the same, irritated by Greene's inconsistency, Ridge found it hard to square his behavior with the avowed fear for Cora which had driven him headlong to come out here from town.

"Do you have to see Turlock?"

"At the earliest possible," she cut in, staring past him as though at something not quite in focus, some elusive thought probably skidding through her head. "Way things are going I've decided to change my will."

Ridge's mouth dropped open. His eyes searched her face.

He wouldn't have imagined a girl young as Cora could have been concerned with such an old man's pastime. In some indefinable way the notion shocked and disturbed him. "I don't think I'd rush into —"

She held up a hand, showed a meagre smile. "Judge Turlock will manage. He's as full of advice as a hen is of feathers. Just tell him I've got to see him right away."

Still staring, Ridge nodded. Though he didn't care much for leaving her alone here he guessed this was as good a means of getting clear of this deal as he would be like to hit on.

"All right," he grunted, taking down his rope. "I'll get right at it."

XVII

It was midafternoon and close as hell's backlog when Ridge came into Clifton with his mind made up. He'd go seek out the judge, give him Cora's message, slip round and pick up those packets of banknotes, then head for the border by the shortest route.

Though not entirely satisfied with this, he had pretty well managed to convince himself that what happened to the girl was not his concern.

She'd got herself into whatever was brewing before Benny'd ever dumped those green and gold engravings onto the Cliff House's spread-covered bed. Why should Ridge feel responsible for her? Just this morning with all of youth's arrogance hadn't she defined his job with her outfit as doing whatever she told him to do? So, all right, he'd do it! He'd give Turlock the message and wash his hands of her.

Just the same he kept wondering what part of her will she was fixing to change and why all the lather to change it right now. On account of Greene's experience or because of her own? Was she taking something out of it or putting something in?

When he found the place, Turlock's office was closed. But the gunsmith next door said the judge had returned and like enough was at home resting up from the trip. "Ain't as spry as he used to be — but, hell, who is?"

He told Ridge how to get there and, five minutes later, stepping through the squeaky gate in the whitewashed picket fence Ridge pulled the bell and heard a distant jangle. When nothing more happened he pulled it again. Approaching footsteps presently loudened down the length of a hall.

When the door was pulled open Ridge found himself eyeing a tousle-haired old man in dressing robe and carpet slippers whose liver-spotted face peered at him with about as much welcome as a fiddler could expect from the keeper of the Pearly Gates.

"I don't do business at home," he gruffed, preparing to shut the door.

But Ridge got a boot in. "Miz Kelly at Tadpole wants you straightaway."

"What for?"

"Something about her will she wants changed."

"Told her 'twas a damfool thing when

she done it," Turlock growled in a dyspeptic grumble. He looked at Ridge sharply. "Ain't sick, is she?"

"She could get that way awful quick," Ridge answered. "Three-four days ago somebody took a shot at her. An' last night that feller she's fixin' to marry got chased up into the mountains by five waddies with rifles."

The old man blinked, rubbing his chin with a fist. "Might have knowed coming in here the way he done, a rank outsider, would turn more than one of these locals against him once it got out he was aimin' to snatch the queen bee off her nest. Well —" he heaved a great sigh, "I'll have the buggy fetched round and get right out there soon's I git myself hitched together."

"You think that's all it is? Somebody tryin' to throw a fright into them?"

"I look like the Oracle of Delphi?" the old judge snorted, and shut the door.

Getting back in the saddle, sundry bits and pieces of this conversation commenced to buzz through Ridge's cogitations, particularly the part where Turlock had snarled *Told her 'twas a damfool thing when she done it.* Had this referred to the making of Cora's will as a whole or to some special part of that document?

But wondering was for numps who sat in rockers and had no better use for their time, he reminded himself, and headed for the Cliff House to pick up his cached stake.

The dust-hazed air was about as hot as the hinges with the heeled-over sun beating into this canyon and Ridge, mopping his face, reckoned he'd better put some thought into how he was to get at it. If the room was still occupied he might have to wait till the tenant went out to fork food to his tapeworm.

He cut away from the street to hunt the hotel's back door which he presently discovered opened onto an alley. Leaving his claybank on grounded reins he pushed open the door and found himself in the kitchen, but the help was too busy to give him much notice as he stepped through a second door into the dining room. A baldheaded man with a star on his vest stood in the lobby arch chewing a matchstick and looking him over with a speculative probe as Ridge, tramping past, coolly headed for the stairs.

He could feel the badge's stare all the way up to the turn at the landing and might have been longer, stopped before the door with the sweat standing cold on his lip, had the screaky treads not heralded the ascending weight of another climber.

Ridge's fisted knuckles rattled the door and getting no response, grasping the knob, shoved it open. Closing it after him he looked quickly around. The room wasn't occupied, the bed freshly made. Not pausing to learn where that climber was headed he crossed to the bureau, lifted it away, and blindly stared at the shape of his cache still plain in the dust on those bare empty boards.

The only thing he could hear in that terrible quiet was the thump of his heart.

Meanwhile back at the ranch Cheeko Morgan, riding into the yard, pulled up with an oath when he sighted the buggy hitched by the gallery fronting the house. He knew straightaway whose it was and, blackly scowling, kicked his horse toward the cook shack, calling Coosie impatiently.

With flour on his hands the cook stuck his head out.

"What's that old fool doin' here?" Morgan rasped.

"I ain't been told."

"Where's that hardcase Cora put on the payroll?"

"Went off someplace on that Anchor Bar

claybank. Thought you was fixin' to —"

"You ain't paid to think!" Morgan growled, and the offended pot wrangler went back to slamming things around inside.

The Tadpole boss rode his mount to the bunkhouse and, leaving it saddled on hanging reins, went inside where he stayed till he heard Turlock's buggy depart. Whereupon he swung back into his hull and crossed the dusty yard to the house.

Perhaps the girl heard him coming. Before he could get out of his stirrups she said, starting from behind the warped screen: "Yes?"

"What'd Turlock want?"

Her mouth fell open. He saw the flush on her cheeks, the angry change in that darkening stare. "Really!" Her chin came up just the way her old man's had. "I don't believe that's any of your business."

"You send that gunfighter after him?"

"What gives you the right to question what I do?"

"Now," he smiled, wheedling, "don't git on yer high hoss. Anything concerns this spread concerns me — you know I got your best interests at heart, Cora. You git a yen fer advice you don't hev t' go all the way to Clifton. I ain't never steered you wrong yet, hev I?"

Less firmly she said, "It hadn't a thing to do with range matters."

"Legal advice, eh?" The man's eyes narrowed. "You fixin' t' git yerself shut of that gunslinger?"

Eyes searching his face she asked, "Why are you so stubborn set against Butler? It's not as if he was after your job — I'd never give him that. If my welfare's really so much in your mind I should think you'd want someone round to look after me —"

"I kin look after you — been doin' it, ain't I? This guy smells to me like a Shackleford spy!"

"Aren't you forgetting how —"

"I ain't fergittin' a goddam thing. Whole deal was hatched up t' git that pelican in here."

"You're wrong," Cora told him. "It couldn't possibly have been. Butler's almost as distrustful of Orren as you are. He thinks Orren was back of those men who chased Billy —"

"He could damn well be right!" Morgan leaned across the brass horn of his saddle, the muscular swell of dark chest and hunched shoulders reminding the girl, with that scowl on his face, of a glowering vulture. "You git rid of that ranny you won't

147

need no pertection. You mark my words: That feller's a killer!"

The girl plainly shivered, and looked off beyond him. "This country is filled with men who have killed. One more won't make any great deal of difference. I'm not firing him anyway. For Greene or you or anyone else."

XVIII

Gone. All gone — every last scrap of it!

Too stunned to curse, Ridge stood with dropped jaw, mind numbly clamped like the gears of a stopped clock to the horrible awareness of his catastrophic loss.

The inexorable advance of booted feet outside, drifting through the grip of this, jolted him into abrupt realization; and his desperate glance, shuttling over the room, was drawn toward the glare of that half-opened window overlooking the street.

With nowhere else to go he still had the wit to set the chest of drawers back against the wall before crouching over to thrust a leg across the sill. Even as he balanced there, scanning what could be glimpsed of the traffic below, the banging of a fist shook authoritative sound from the panels of the door.

Hauling the other leg after him Ridge dropped the few feet to the verandah's shingled roof, feeling the lurch of it beneath his weight. Wasting no time looking to see if he were watched he hurried to the corner of the high false front, slithering gingerly around it to go scrabbling his way across the steep pitch in a mindless race for the alley behind.

But the Anchor Bar claybank was no longer there.

Afraid now of the alley, shaken out of his freeze by the shouts from below, he slanched a wild look at the rooftops about him.

"He's up there!" someone yelled avidly and Ridge, without further prod, made a frantic leap only inches short, to dangle by the convulsed grip of fingers from the eaves of the building next in line.

Prizing himself up through the roar from below, rolling onto his knees to scramble over the ridge-tree, he slid down the far slope, managing to curb his momentum sufficiently to hurl himself across the next gap and land spraddled out behind the foot-high parapet of a flat topped adobe.

But there his luck appeared to change.

While he debated dropping over the side his swiveling glance fastened onto a hatch-covered trap not ten feet away. But the thing, while shifting beneath his pull, refused to come up. He kicked it savagely, swearing in frustration; and whatever had been anchoring it did so no longer. Tossing the cover aside he dropped through the

150

hole to a teetering table in the room below, lunging clear as it capsized, accompanied by a woman's rising scream as he whirled toward a door.

Wrenching it open he stared into a closet shared by old boots with a single hung dress. Twisting round, his bitter glance dug the street door from a gloom deep with shadows. Before he could reach it the woman was onto him, belaboring him with a cracked old maleta, screeching abuse like a straddle-house trollop. Flinging her aside Ridge yanked open the door, teeth bared in a snarl as he hauled it shut after him, holding it that way while his eyes scoured the street.

Except for abandoned rigs the nearby vicinity was practically deserted, the bulk of those who had witnessed his gymnastics having rushed at full cry toward the backs of the buildings. Only two of the teams still had drivers and both, in the excitement, were watching the rooftops. Two doors away, before a saloon, five hitched horses were switching flies.

Curbing his impatience Ridge drifted toward them like a waddy unable to make up his mind whether he wanted a drink or not. Last thing he did want was to attract the drivers' attention. He kept his eyes off them, sizing up the horses.

Time he got to the hitch rail he'd decided which of the bunch looked most likely and, ducking under it, pulled loose the reins of a buckskin showing squiggles of darker hair above and below the knees — a bayo coyote with a dark dorsal stripe. With the animal's head pulled toward him Ridge thrust a boot in the stirrup, and was just settling into the saddle when a man — coming through the batwings — took one shocked look and reached for his shooter.

"You!" he yelled; but Ridge had the horse spun clear by then and, urged by his steel, had the buckskin going like a cougar was after him when the fellow, barreling to where nothing stood in his way, angrily banged all the loads from his pistol.

Since none of those slugs came within a yard of him, Ridge — leaving town on the Guthrie road — reckoned the man had been afraid of cutting down his own mount. But this didn't mean he wouldn't give chase.

Ridge was more worried about that galoot with the star and what had become of the Anchor Bar claybank he'd left in the alley. The badge packer, if he was the one who'd followed Ridge up the stairs, wouldn't have had time to mess around with the horse. And without he found out who the claybank belonged to it wasn't too likely, Ridge reminded himself, the man would have any leads at all. Unless the owner of this bayo coyote had waited around back there for help.

Rationalization did very little for an empty belly, and no amount of cogitating could take away the weighted look which had trailed Ridge up those hotel stairs.

Where brush grew thick along the dusty road he wheeled the buckskin through a break and swung down to stand by the pony's head deep within a juniper thicket. If that fellow'd lit out on the nearest mount he should be racking past inside a handful of seconds. And sure enough, almost at once Ridge caught the sound of a fast traveling horse.

Not till this racket had gotten well past did Ridge lift clamped grip from the animal's muzzle and climb back aboard, there to sit half a minute toting up where the loss of that cache had put him. Without Benny's dollars he was back where he'd started, too old for this game and too strapped to quit.

After swinging back into the north via a wide and antigodlin loop that took him hours out of the way, Ridge entered Tadpole country from the west through a region as desolate and rough, he thought, as any he had yet encountered — all ups and downs that were gouged and split by countless gullies, creating such a maze that he wondered several times if he were going round in circles. He had never seen anything like it. Fenced in by towering red rock cliffs and shale strewn cul-de-sacs given over to catclaw and pear, it looked fit for nothing but javelinas and snakes, though he did occasionally jump frightened jacks that were no more startled by the confrontation than he was.

He got so weary in the dark trying to find a way out he finally pulled the gear off the horse and, after hobbling the animal Indian fashion, got under the saddle blanket and tried to catch some rest.

Despite empty belly and a swatch of anxieties persistent as gadflies he must eventually have dozed. The sun was up and the hobbled horse was whimpering next time he twisted onto an elbow.

Throwing off the pungent wool, aided by an assortment of groans and cuss words, he succeeded in extending enough protesting muscles to get himself afoot. The surroundings did not look much improved by details revealed in the sun's early light. The view was still desolate, only now there was more of it. He could tell east from west, which was more than he'd been sure of last night.

He was moving, still groggy, toward the purloined horse when his swiveling glance caught a sidelong impression of a motionless shape keeping tabs on his progress. His arrested look took in the long ears and twitching nose, and the pistol recoiled against the heel of his hand. A few minutes later he had a meager fire going and was cutting up the luckless rabbit for breakfast. Damn thing was half raw from dearth of fuel but Ridge could have gulped down three more just like it. Right then he guessed he could have eaten a coyote had any come round to pop into his sights.

It was while he was cleaning his knife of the blood that his attention was drawn to some faint scintillation emanating from an outcrop a dozen yards away. Curiosity presently took him nearer to find it came from a darker mottling in the crevice of the rock. At first he took it to be some sort of moss — it was that kind of green, but when he scratched at it with the point of his knife a breath of excitement got into his interest and he broke off a small chunk, lips pursed in a whistle as a hunch began of a sudden to take shape.

The whole exposed surface was shot full of color, weathering out as bits crumbled away. Now he recalled where he'd seen this before. It appeared identical to the roughly polished bola used by Cheeko Morgan to hold the hatstrings together beneath that Neanderthal jaw.

Scowling, Ridge stuffed the chunk in shirt pocket and spent half an hour looking at other rocks in the area, trying to fit this thing into the over-all picture. The stuff wasn't jade — that much he was sure of. He didn't know a heap about mining or minerals but thought the material not nearly blue enough for turquoise. Whatever it was there certainly appeared to be plenty of it.

He piled the gear on the horse and, still engrossed, cinched up. Lifting a leg to thrust boot in stirrup he saw that he hadn't yet removed the pony's hobbles. With a snort he reckoned he'd better get his wits about him, and, suddenly uneasy, threw a quick look around before bending down to cut the ropes loose.

It was the quiet that bothered him, the kind of stillness a man associated with Apaches; and he peered again, probing each patch of shadow, glance sweeping the rim-rocks without sighting anything to account for raised hackles.

He started once more to get into the saddle and, like the fist of a giant, something slammed into his chest just below the left nipple. A million lights exploded in his head. Then the lights went out. He felt himself falling down a black spiral that grew steadily darker.

XIX

It was midafternoon and some five miles east of where he'd been dropped before Ridge was able by waving both arms to catch at the notice of a distant rider.

He felt some qualms about attracting this attention, but hours afoot irritably tended to fray the stay ropes of a man's natural bent and, besides, to make no bones of it, Butler was pooped.

The fellow turned out to be one of Morgan's Tadpole crew. When he came up, stare taking in Ridge's disheveled, half-baked appearance, he said sloe-eyed, "You git caught in a twister?"

"Something like that."

"What happened to yer hoss?"

"Got spooked an' dumped me." Ridge asked grimly, "How about giving me a lift to the ranch?"

The horsebacker shot a dubious look at the sun. "Kinda early fer quittin' . . . not sure Cheeko'd like it."

"I'll fix that," Ridge grunted, palming his pistol. "You want to walk or ride double?"

"You got *me* convinced." Through a

parched smile the man kicked loose of an oxbow, giving Ridge a hand up.

Half an hour later, with no further talk, they rode into the Tadpole yard where Ridge, dropping off, growled, "Obliged," and headed for the house.

There was no need to knock because Cora, with some sewing, was occupying a chair in the shade of the gallery. With an expression of surprise she waited out his approach. "What happened to your horse?"

"Somebody, seemed like, wasn't downright anxious to see me quit town," Ridge answered, looking her over; and went on to recount the manner of his leaving.

She said with concern: "Don't you think that was just a little brash? Going off, I mean, on another man's horse?"

"It was one of them times when discretion looked the healthier part of valor. Wouldn't of been much good to you shot or —"

"What were you doing in the hotel anyway?"

"Personal business."

She could see from tone and look he wasn't about to enlarge on the matter. "You think it was Rondecker moved your horse?"

"Don't know any Rondecker."

"The marshal," she said.

Anger showed in his look. "I don't know about that, but it's a leadpipe cinch someone pointed him at me. He never come up them stairs after me just to pass the time of day."

Something slipped through her glance like doubt. She shrugged it away to ask, "What do you figure to do if a posse —"

"Huntin' horse thieves ain't a town marshal's job. This place is outside his bailiwick and what tracks I left is too scrambled up to fetch *anyone* here." He stood for a couple of frowning breaths, staring, then dug from shirt pocket the chunk of rock he'd pried loose and dropped it into her hand. "What do you reckon this is?"

Apparently puzzled she turned the thing over, shaking her head. "Looks like a piece of rock . . . you mean that shiny streak?" She peered more intently. "Is it silver?"

"Track of a lead plum — look at the rock. Ever see anything like it?"

"I'm not . . . I don't think so." She looked up reluctantly out of gray cheeks, then stared again at the mark on the rock. "You been shooting at targets?"

"Somebody has. Same one probably

choused Rondecker onto me. Same feller, I'd guess, that was gunning for you."

He said rather grimly: "Except for this chunk of rock in my pocket he might damn well have got me. Probably reckons he did or he'd have stopped to make sure. That stuff's on your range." He described its location. "Looks like the same kind of rock your range boss is wearin' to keep the hat on his noggin."

There was a grayer color in the cant of her cheeks and her eyes looked the shade of smoky sage. He could not in this light decipher their expression, could not be sure if what he saw were fright or worry. He had a halfway thought that what she was hiding might actually be anger and said, impatient: "Get your thinkin' cap on! Don't this tell you a goddam thing?"

She considered him uneasily, watching him out of that wooden face. "I can see you think this rock might have value." A desperate smile ran across pale lips. She lifted slim shoulders, let them drop with a sigh. "I guess you think I should be finding out."

When his beard stubbled face stayed bleakly shut she got out of the chair, put down her sewing, coming nearer to stand where the sun's dying shafts kicked up sorrel tints in the mass of her hair. One hand crept out to touch his arm. With that hard-to-read look, scarcely louder than a whisper, she tensely said, "There are times a woman would almost rather be deceived than see things as they truly are."

And sighed again, letting go of him. "Who could we trust to discover its worth?"

"Couldn't Turlock take it to some reliable assayer?"

"Judge is in Clifton. *You* can't go. Who'd make the trip? You want me —"

"That's out," he guffed.

"Then we'll have to send one of the hands —"

"Why not Cheeko?"

Cora peered at him, startled. "But I thought —"

"Good way to find out."

Their eyes searched each other through a lengthening stillness.

The girl's shoulders moved. With a trace of impatience she shook her head. "I don't think —"

"He does his job. Puts the brand's best interests —"

Through a flush she said, "But you don't trust him. Neither does Billy. And, if you're right, he's using a piece of this rock for a bola. If he's behind whatever is going on around here —"

"That's just the point. One way or another —" Ridge broke off to listen, threw a look toward the lane. "There's your outfit now. Get him over here."

She chewed at her lip. "It wouldn't be a fair test —"

"Who cares about fair?" Ridge growled at her roughly. "Haven't you got it through your head yet somebody's out to clobber this outfit? Somebody wants you dead and buried!"

XX

It was evident from her expression she couldn't really believe it even now. When Ridge snorted she squinted her eyes to peer again at the rock. "And you think this is back of it . . . that someone wants this bad enough to kill for it?"

"What else is there *to* think? Whoever took that potshot at me sure didn't have *my* best interests in mind! Somebody don't want you marryin' Greene. Whoever it is may not know about this. But it's my guess he does, an' will do whatever comes handiest to make damn sure he winds up with it. This rock ain't something that's just popped up; it's been weatherin' out for a good many years. Thing is, until now no one seems to've got wind of it. I'd say this vinegaroon aims to take over before someone else does."

"And you want Morgan to learn we both know about it?"

"Right now we've got a Mexican standoff. I want to prod this galoot into showin' his hand." He gave her a slanchways, considering look. "You ain't got much time left. This stuff may be worthless, may have nothing to do with them slugs thrown at us. Best way to find out is to get a report on this."

"If Morgan's the man and we send this stone by him, telling him what's up or sending a note with it, you don't believe it will —"

"If Cheeko's the one he's going to have to do something. And almighty quick."

The sun dropped below the west rim. Swiftly the yard began to fill up with shadows. The girl said, watching, "If I do what you want, and you're right about Morgan, won't he try to get rid of you?"

"Don't let it keep you awake," Ridge grinned.

"And if you're wrong?"

"We'll take a sample to Orren."

With an obvious repugnance the girl said, "I don't like it. My father believed in shooting straight from the shoulder —"

"Your father's dead. You hankerin' to join him?"

"Just the same," she cried, "it's underhanded, *dirty!*"

"Whole deal is dirty. You ain't playing jacks, Cora. You've got your life on the line and you better believe it."

She looked eye-flashing angry. "I'm not going to do it!"

Ridge blew out his breath and pawed at his face, hand rasping harshly across bristly jowls. "Listen," he growled. "I came into this country hunting a stake. I was sent for, promised a big wad of cash. All I had to do is get rid of a rancher. Case you don't know, it was C. L. Kelly."

"But that's . . ." She stared, speechless, the enormity of what he'd just said sinking into her. Disbelief, horror, distorted her cheeks; and she backed off a step, hand pushed out before her. She moistened pale lips but before she could speak Ridge, twisting his head to seek the source of fresh hoof sound, grunted, "Shackleford!" and cursed.

Coosie picked that moment to pound a racket from his wreckpan. "Come an' git it, you hawgs, afore I throw it away!"

As the crew went dragging their spurs toward the sound the Anchor Bar owner, apparently discovering the pair in the shadows, reined his mount toward the gallery. He must have sensed the tension between them for — stopping the horse a few feet away — his glance went from girl to man and back again, narrowing. "I trust," he murmured, "I'm not interrupting something?"

"Of course not," the girl answered, surfacing from shock with an obvious effort, finally hauling her look from Ridge's face to say, "Do get down, Orren, and find yourself a chair. Have you eaten?"

"Too early for me." Shackleford stepped down, let go of the reins, and — still eyeing Ridge — settled himself in a hide-bottomed rocker. "Well," he said, "have you got any nearer to finding that feller?"

Ridge shrugged, grimly silent, but looked around sharply when Cora Lee said in a determined tone of voice, "Ridge is on the list now. This morning, while riding those roughs south of Crenshaw's, he was knocked off his horse and left there for dead."

Orren Shackleford whistled. "You get a look at him, Butler?"

The girl picked it up before Ridge could answer. "If you'll step across and fetch Morgan from his supper, I believe I've something both of you should hear."

Shackleford considered the expression on her face and, nodding, got up without remark to strike off across the darkening yard. Ridge, graveled and glaring, angrily waited for him to get out of earshot before saying harshly: "Are you out of your mind?"

She said defiantly, "They've a right to be told."

She must have seen his cramped look, sensed the churning thoughts back of it. Ridge got hold of himself. "If this stuff has any value at all you're opening the way for a string of claims —"

"Perhaps you'd better rush out there and file! If you haven't already!" She peered at him bleakly. "Throwing this open looks the only sane answer I'm like to come up with. Go on — grab a horse and get whacking if you don't want to be caught up in the stampede. Or did you intend to take care of me first?" Watching him with an open contempt she drove the barb in to where he could feel it. "You might not find it so easy to collect for my scalp once this discovery becomes common property."

"What do you want me to do," Ridge growled, "apologize because you turned out to be a female? If all you're doin' this for's to spite *me* you're flingin' away this spread's best potential."

"Tadpole is cows," she said with her chin up. "If you're really laying off to put a star in your crown, why not put a name to the polecat that hired you?"

Looked for a minute he was too riled to answer. He finally said "I don't know who hired me. Job came my way from a Dallas attorney."

Whatever she might have said to that was cut off by the approach of Shackleford and a bristling Cheeko. Wheeling, the girl called over her shoulder, "Fetch them inside," and went off to get a lamp lit.

Ridge felt an urge to go catch up a horse, but stood his ground, scowling. "You're wanted inside," he told the pair when they joined him.

"What's this about?" the rancher asked.

"She's about to cut her throat," Ridge grunted, waving them sourly on toward the door.

Shackleford took another look at him before following the range boss into the house.

In the lamplit room with its Navajo rugs and mounted trophies to her old man's skill with a rifle, Cora Lee said, "I want you to take a good look at this rock," and put it down on the table, Morgan and the rancher crowding round her to look, Ridge standing watchful by the still open door. "Can either of you tell what it is?"

Morgan said without interest, "Looks the same kinda stone I've got for a bola."

There was no change at all on Shackleford's face, though Ridge thought his stare might have grown a bit sharper. "Orren?" Cora said, and the Anchor Bar owner gave a short nod. "Looks like a piece of variscite to me. Where'd it come from?"

"Butler stumbled onto it. Says he broke it off an outcrop this morning."

"Around here?" Orren asked, glance swinging to Ridge.

"On Tadpole range," Cora quietly answered. "South of Crenshaw. Does it have any value?"

Shackleford, eyes hooded, cleared his throat. "I'd say offhand seven fifty an ounce. If it's all like this chunk." He twisted around to throw another scowl at Ridge.

Before Ridge — if he'd intended to — was able to decide how much to reveal, Cheeko Morgan said hotly: "That why you been layin' pipe to take this spread over?"

Cora, as color suffused the rancher's cheeks, cried, "We'll have no more of that! I've decided to share this discovery. We'll go out there tomorrow and we'll each of us stake claims —"

Morgan growled, furious, "Why should you give away any part of it? If it's in them roughs it belongs —"

Cora said flatly, "I don't particularly

relish being shot at. If we each have a share I don't imagine I'll prove quite so tempting a target."

As they considered each other in shock's brittle silence Ridge thought the rancher looked a shade the more startled by the girl's blunt words. But it was Morgan that said in a half-teasing drawl, "I doubt even Orren would go that far, Cora. He was just tryin' to throw a little scare into you."

Shackleford looked his contempt of so snide an assertion, but his whole stance tightened when the girl quietly said, "I don't believe Butler's going to buy that, Cheeko. On his own confession he came into this country on a contract to kill me."

XXI

The stares of both men surged against Butler's, outraged, probing, trying to read what lay back of those inscrutable cheeks. Morgan, almost beside himself snarled. Shackleford, obviously shaken, was showing his age. The Tadpole boss, from a livid, black-patched countenance, cried: "What are we waitin' on? All we need's a wagon tongue an' a rope —"

"There'll be none of that here!" Cora Lee proclaimed sharply.

"You're not aiming to turn him loose?" Shackleford demanded, astonished. "Only a mad dog would engage to kill a woman!"

"He'd no way of knowing C. L. Kelly was a woman — they never told him." She said anxiously then, "I've promised he'll go with us tomorrow, free to stake —"

Morgan said hotly, "That's the craziest thing outa you I've heard yet!" and Shackleford nodded. "Forgiveness surely is one of woman's noblest virtues but I'll remind you, my dear, that coddling a viper is not without hazard. You'd do better to leave men's business —"

"Somewhere I seem to have heard that before." Cora's chin tilted rebelliously.

"Where's Greene?" Cheeko growled. "He know what you're up to?"

Orren Shackleford said, "I'd be more interested in learning who put Butler up to this."

"He doesn't know. He got the job from a lawyer —"

"Twopence colored and fivepence shy," the rancher observed as one who could separate the sheep from the goats. "How'd you happen to wangle it out of him — that he came here to kill you?"

Shoulder propped against door frame, Ridge said, "I figured it was time she was made to realize someone round here wants to get rid of her."

Shackleford let that pass with curled lip. "Anyway," Cora slogged on as the pair peered at Ridge, "if we all file claims it won't much matter because the profit incentive . . ."

Morgan, exasperated, threw out both hands. "No bunch of fool rocks is what's back of this!" But Shackleford, smarter, looking hard at the girl, asked: "Am I to understand you believe one of *us* to be the skunk who hired Butler?"

Cora flushed. Ridge said, roughly throwing the words at them, "Who else stands to gain by taking her out of this?" Then, looking straight into Shackleford's glare, "I never run into no cow mogul yet that didn't picture himself bigger than Billy-be-damn.

"Why, you cocky upstart!" Shackleford cried in a half-stranged shout. "I've a good mind —"

"You may have a good mind for doing folks out of things, but when it comes to hoorawin' a growed man, mister, you better stick to hirin' your dirty work done."

With an outraged look in Cora's direction the Anchor Bar owner, mottled jowls trembling, shoved through the door and went over the gallery like a wet-footed cat to haul himself furiously into the saddle. With a saturnine grin, "Sure wouldn't want to be in *his* pony's shoes," Cheeko said through the hard running sound of the rancher's departure. "Reckon we've seen the last of him fer a while!"

"Wouldn't count on it," Ridge grunted. And, to the girl: "You'll notice he knew the name for them rocks, and right to the penny how much they'll bring. Which doesn't," he added with an oblique glance at Morgan, "necessarily prove anything either way. Right now he's uglier than galvanized sin; but if it's him put up that twenty-five hundred to stop Cora travelin' double harness with Greene you can bet top dollar he'll be on tap tomorrow."

The girl said, astonished, "But what could marrying Billy have to do with this?"

"Price was five grand. But unless I took care of you ahead of that weddin' all I could pick up was the come-on dished out by that law shark. Might help," Ridge mentioned, "if you'd say what you had me chouse Turlock out here for."

Seeing Morgan's sharpened look, "I did tell you," she hedged, flushing.

"Only that you figured to change your will — not in which direction."

Morgan, having glimpsed signals Ridge had chosen to ignore, cried in a scowling tone of resentment, "If you're givin' this joker any part of Tadpole —"

"What I do with Tadpole," the girl said through angry cheeks, "is my concern entirely. But just to put your mind at rest I'm not giving any part of Tadpole to *anyone!* Now get out of here, both of you, and give me a little peace!"

Tired as he was, Ridge — having found a dark corner of the yard to bed down in — found his thoughts too furrowed by contradictions to leave any ground for cultivation of sleep. Cora had sure enough opened up a fine kettle of fish when — in trying to protect herself — she'd divulged his reason for coming here. Still, he couldn't really blame her; he should have had better sense than spill his guts that way.

The girl had a head screwed onto her shoulders. It had been a shrewd move to show that rock around, suggesting they all go and stake claims tomorrow. If this variscite turned out to be the springboard under all this, her announcement of its discovery and offer to share it should spike the guns of whoever had commissioned that shyster to hire him. Not much point in killing her for something turned loose of her control. Feller would be smarter to abandon his schemes and grab what he could in that frolic tomorrow. Whoever was back of this deal against Cora stood damn little chance now of cornering the lot.

Despite the variscite Cheeko wore as a clamp for the strings of his blue sombrero, Ridge couldn't think there was a heap besides hair hidden under the hat. But knowing how deceptive appearances could be he was not yet ready to give Morgan a clean bill. The man was a blowhard, a bullypuss and bluffer, but this *could* be an act; he could prove underneath that flamboyant exterior to be as tough-minded and ambitious as the glib little bantam who had parlayed his holdings into the outfit called Anchor Bar. Through these twistings and turnings it did not escape Butler, despite Cheeko's rantings, that the pair of them might be in this together, each of them maneuvering to grab the winning hand.

And what about Greene? Where in tarnation was the man at now? Was he going to miss out on tomorrow's scramble or was the girl aiming to get a string of claims staked for him? With all he had going for him down there in Florida, Ridge guessed Billy wouldn't head for the poorhouse if he did get left out; though it did sort of drift through Ridge's mind that that chase the other night might just have decided him to cut his string or at the least to hunt some place where they couldn't get at him.

He was a heap more concerned, though, with his own immediate prospects. With that contract money furnished by Benny gone up the spout he would soon be back to scrounging drinks if he couldn't in some fashion make a strike quick. This variscite deal looked a long-winded while short of paying any bills. Unless . . .

It was this new notion which drove any likelihood of sleep from his head. A man had to be ready for a string of spools if he figured to be snapping any caps at Cora now. But if these claims could be unloaded for cash — even at a measly fifty cents on the dollar, a feller might make at least get-away money. Sell them back to the girl or — Hell's fire! Of course! Who would pay more than the son of a bitch who'd been aiming all along to grab off the whole works!

But two hours of trying to guess which of them it was got him not a whit further than he'd been when he came here. Ridge was still wrestling with it when sleep overtook him.

Departure of the crew bound for the chores laid out for them by Morgan roused Ridge groggily at day's first light, and he got stiffly out of his soogans to peer blearily about without discovering anything to pleasure the warmed-over thoughts on which he'd been pounding his ear. Morgan, chewing a matchstick, stepped from the cook shack to give him a slanchways, ugly look before striking off at a saddle-bound swagger in the general direction of the pole corrals.

Something occurred to Ridge then which — while it certainly hadn't escaped his notice — he now began to feel had got too little of his attention. That matter of Cora changing her will, or at least fetching Turlock all the way out here for that declared purpose. It seemed to him now to hold strong significance — particularly since, it suddenly appeared, she hadn't intended her range boss to know of it.

With increasing curiosity his thoughts began to push and poke at the notion. Why had she changed it — or *had* she? And what new development had shoved her into thinking she ought to? Even more to the point, just what change had she contemplated? If he could see or find out what she'd had in mind he had a hunch this whole deal might look a lot different.

Peering toward the house he took off for the cook shack. Didn't seem a heap likely she'd tell if he asked, a conviction which only served to whet his interest. Why had the decision suddenly moved her to wake and send the man she'd hired for protection galivanting hotfoot all those up-and-down miles to Clifton? And the snorted remark it had got from the judge. *Told her 'twas a damfool thing when she done it.*

Coosie said when Ridge appeared in the

doorway, "You think I got nothin' better t' do than dish up handouts —"

"I didn't come here for gab. Rustle your butt and fix me some grub. An' don't waste my time standin' round looking raunchy."

The scowling cook had his lip up a foot when the color of Ridge's stare set him back on his haunches and spun him snarling toward the stove where he set up a mean-faced clatter as he slammed pots onto the still warm lids.

"Better kick up that fire — I ain't got all day."

A rumor of hoof-sound rolled through the shack as Ridge tied into the grub Coosie'd flung down before him, but he went on with his eating when a glance through the door showed Morgan crossing the yard with a brace of saddled mounts. He didn't think it too likely they would set off without him. Cheeko — if he knew where to go — would hardly tip his hand with proof of the fact.

Ridge washed down the food with an extra mug of Arbuckle, dragged a sleeve across his chin and went and got down his rope, neatly forefooting a snorting sorrell-maned dun. It was while he was piling his gear on the horse that further hoof-plopping pulled around his jaw to discover Orren Shackleford bound across the yard toward where Morgan stood flapping his lip at the girl.

XXII

The claim-staking excursion was at least un-
marred by any outbreak of violence, despite
short tempers and frequent black scowls. At
Cora's suggestion the three men drew straws
for choice of location after it was settled that
a total of four claims would be the limit for
each. Oddly enough, it was Ridge who
wound up getting first choice.

Although he privately wondered if this
were bull luck or some deliberate artifice
engineered by the girl, he didn't let the
suspicion prevent him from including the
outcrop and what looked to be the best
ground all around. Shackleford, second to
get his pick, took the most likely adjoining
parcels. Cora staked third and a fuming
Morgan went stomping around to claim
what was left.

"Might be wise," Orren pointed out, "for
one of us to camp here until these claims
are on record." But Cora didn't seem to really care for the notion and no one felt
brash enough to carry it further.

A dearth of conversation marked the
homeward trip; and it wasn't until along

into the darkening shank of the evening, as they pulled into the yard at Cora's head-quarters, that Ridge, clearing his throat, declared, "I've about as much use for these claims as a bull has for bloomers." Letting that sink in, he casually added, "If I was to get a fair offer guess I'd let the whole lot go," and kneed his mount toward the clutter of pens.

"Hold on!" Morgan growled. "We ain't settled yet who's to ride in an' file. Ain't the kinda thing we ought to put off fer long."

Shackleford said, "What's wrong with each of us filing his own?"

Morgan threw him a scowl. "Why don't we git us a bit to eat, catch up fresh ponies an' set out fer the county seat straight-away?"

"Can't see much point to it," Shackleford murmured after glancing at Cora. "It's not as though we didn't trust each other . . . or did you think one of us might just be fixing to gobble the whole damn kit and caboodle?"

"I wouldn't put it past you!" Cheeko said straight out.

Shackleford laughed.

Cora passed round an anxious glance. "Let's not spoil this whole thing now. Considering Butler's views on the subject, why not delegate him to file for all of us?"

"Suits me," Orren nodded.

"Well, it don't suit *me*," flared Morgan hotly.

Cora's mobile features showed her exasperation. Shackleford said in an amused tone of voice, "I'm thankful not to have been put together with what was left over when they got around to you."

The tawny eye in Cheeko's darkening face showed the rolling white of a stallion bronc. With a spread right hand he was hunched to erupt when the girl cried angrily, "It was to avoid this kind of thing I made up my mind to share this find. You can each of you do whatever you want, but don't expect *me* to spend the night in a saddle!"

"I reckon," Ridge nodded, "I can wait until mornin'," and heeled his horse corralwards again. It was like to be risky going in at all, but the girl's needs and worries had no part in this decision; he wanted to give the bait time enough to bear fruit, confident that before another day dawned one of the pair would have made him an offer. Perhaps the proposition wouldn't come from Benny's client, though the reasons for this hunch rather tended to assure him no one else would feel so pushed.

With his horse taken care of he came back across a yard now mottled with lamplight, intending before he dug out his blankets to have a look at what Coosie had dished up for the crew.

Cora stepped out of the dark to intercept him.

"Orren's spending the night. Try if you can to keep Cheeko away from him. The way he's been acting —"

"Morgan's no kid, Cora."

"But he's so bull headed. . . ." She put a hand on his arm; he could feel it tremble, felt the nearness of the girl washing through him like a belt of white lightning. And yanked himself away, lips twisted in a curse, to cry at her hoarsely, "Why'd you leave Greene out of this?"

He could feel the hard search of her look focused on him. "What else could I do? He wasn't around —"

"You could certainly have waited till you was able to get hold of him. Something wrong between you two?"

"Of course not," she said; but too quickly, he thought, and threw at her roughly: "You call off that weddin'?"

"Now what put that idea in your head?"

"You been actin' damn odd ever since that night I found him in the house after lookin' all over —"

"Your concern does you credit," she said with chin up, "but it's plain you've let imagination run away with you. If I've seemed distracted it's because I'm just about frantic with worry. I simply can't understand —"

"Is the weddin' called off?"

"Of course it's not."

He stood a brief while eyeing her through the shadows, disturbed and dissatisfied yet not quite able to pin down the nuances he felt in her tone. He blew out his cheeks. She was probably right and he was reading too much into things which held no hidden significance. Jumping to conclusions could play queer tricks and — given enough rein — turn black into white if a man didn't watch himself.

With pulse still thumping like some muted drum he clamped down on his emotions, shoulders moving in a shrug as his glance wheeled again across that vibrant shape. "I'll not ride herd on any man," he grunted, "but if Morgan . . ."

"Yes." She sighed. "That's all I ask."

Ridge stood there frowning long after her shape had disappeared in the shadows

186

— and was there, still wondering, when Shackleford said back of him, "About those claims . . . how much cash would it take to move you out of this?"

XXIII

Butler, turning, showed a mirthless grin. "How high you want to go?"

"Name your price."

"All I can get."

"Would twenty-five hundred take you out of these parts?"

Like a bell the words clanged through Ridge's head. He pulled in a deep breath. "How much you offering for that block of claims?"

Shackleford gave the short bark of a laugh. "Don't push your luck. Lot of powder can be burnt for that kind of money."

"If you don't run into a blue whistler someplace."

They considered each other through a slow run of seconds. Ridge's lips twisted in a grimace of mockery. The cowman said impatiently, "Three thousand for the claims and —"

"Don't set up conditions you're not able to enforce."

The man chewed at his cheek. "Will you take three thousand?"

"I was offered five just to rub out that girl."

"I'll go that high if you'll throw in the name —"

"If you don't know that already I'll throw in the claims and go for nothing."

In the explosive silence a shutter banged someplace, caught in a lift of wind off the rim-rocks. Shackleford growled, "You're not going to wipe that crap off on me!"

"Put it this way. How many can you name inside a day's ride that could cough up five grand to get rid of a neighbor?"

"You son of a bitch!" Orren said through his teeth.

Ridge Butler smiled. "Takes hard cash to get rid of a nuisance."

The boss of Anchor Bar stood there flapping like a wash in a wind till Ridge drawled, "Watch that blood pressure, Orren."

When he was able to speak the cowman said in a half-strangled growl: "After you've recorded those locations tomorrow and made out a quitclaim properly witnessed and notarized, there'll be three thousand waiting at the teller's cage at the Clifton Bank. And if you want more than that you know where to stuff them!"

"I'll be there," Ridge nodded.

He went on to the cook shack and filled

a plate, then went back to pour a mugful of java, black and strong enough to float anything that wasn't nailed down. Most of the crew had already left. When Ridge had eaten he stepped outside to roll a smoke, then crossed to the bunkhouse and picked up his blankets. Outside again he found Morgan waiting. "If you got a spare moment I'd like to habla with you," said the Tadpole boss in a gravelly voice.

Ridge dropped the quirly and put a boot on it. "Go right ahead."

"Over here," the man grunted, and pulled up in the darkest center of the yard. Ridge with both eyes peeled stopped there beside him, waiting while Cheeko bit a chaw from a nub of Cable twist. After chomping till he had it shaped up to his satisfaction the range boss spat, saying from the other side of his mouth, "How much you askin' fer them four claims?"

Ridge looked him over. "What'll you give?"

The man said, scowling, "Money don't grow on the brush round here. Give you five hundred bucks, half the profits an' do all the work. How's that sound?"

"A bit on the short side. Been offered twenty-five hundred. Cash at the bank."

Morgan, chewing, finally spat. "Shackle

190

ford, eh? You take it?"

"Ain't taken it yet."

Cheeko's jaws ground as though it was Orren's neck between his teeth. "I'd like jist onct t' git ahead of that bastard!"

"Beat his price and the claims are yours."

"Where the hell would I rake up that kinda dough?"

"Your problem," Ridge grunted, waving him off.

"How much time hev I got?"

"Till the Clifton bank shuts its doors tomorrow."

Still Cheeko hesitated, the tone of him astonished. "You figgerin' to pull out?"

"You won't cry over that, will you?" When the man stood in silence, "Feller gets to know when he's wore out his welcome." And, shouldering his roll, Ridge left Morgan standing there.

In the meagre early light of another day Ridge Butler, bent over the horse trough scraping his face, glanced up at the sound of hooves to see Morgan by the farthest corral getting down off a sweat-stained hard-ridden pony.

At about the time Ridge was folding his razor the girl appeared on the gallery, beckoning. When he made out not to notice she came off the planks, quartering over the yard. "Butler!" she called, hurrying her stride. Distrustful, Ridge waited.

"What's this about you fixing to leave?" Her eyes searched his face. "You're not really, are you?"

"I think," he said, "you'll be safe enough now."

"But . . . but . . ." Her head moved impatiently. She looked pretty ruffled, her face showing the pinched tightness of alarm and something else less easily determined. "I don't *want* you to go!" she cried at him angrily.

" 'Fraid you're getting me mixed up with Greene. He'll be looking out for you after tomorrow."

She opened her mouth, then closed it again, holding him with the grip of her stare. "Why do you suppose I put those claims in your way?"

Ridge shook his head. "You're too big a girl to start playin' with fire."

A deeper color suffused her cheeks but her look never wavered. Darker, it stayed on him while she chewed at a lip. "At least you'll stay until after the wedding?"

"All right," he grumbled and, hearing cook banging out the call to breakfast, took off with soap and towel for the bunk-house.

Cheeko Morgan came in while he was putting on his shirt. Without beating around any bushes Morgan said, "From the time he showed up that jigger she's marryin' has stuck in my craw." He fetched a crumpled yellow paper from a pocket, held it out. "Cast your eye over this!"

Ridge smoothed the thing out and read: PER YOUR REQUEST DESCRIPTION BOXED BELL OWNER FIVE ELEVEN BROWN EYES BALD WEIGHT TWO EIGHTY FIVE COMPLEXION FLORID FIRST FINGER LEFT HAND MISS-ING SECOND KNUCKLE NOT CURRENTLY IN RESIDENCE.

Morgan said with curled lip, "That sound t' you like this feller Greene?"

Glancing up from the telegram Ridge considered through a frowning silence to presently ask, peering again at the signa-ture, "Who's Haynes?"

"U.S. Marshal at Kissimmee."

Ridge stood in his tracks. "Just what are you figuring to do with this, Cheeko?"

Morgan put out a hand. "What do you reckon? She goes through with that weddin' I'm out on my ear."

Ridge, ignoring the hand, stuffed the paper in his pocket. "You get that from her?"

Morgan's working eye peered around the hooked nose. "Some things, by God, I don't hev t' be told! Now gimme that paper. When this phoney takes over —"

"When was the last time you saw Greene?"

Scowling, Morgan said, "It was the night after them fellers chased him. Didn't even know the peckerneck was back till noise from the pens fetched me outa my bunk t' see this tinhorn sneakin' a horse out!"

"And hasn't it," Ridge nodded, "seemed to you like Cora's been acting just a mite odd —"

"You mean them two's had some kinda set-to?"

"I expect there's been words passed. Woke me up next morning. Nothing would do but I must get on a horse and go foggin' to town like school wouldn't keep another ten minutes without the judge got himself straight out here."

"Yeah," Morgan grumbled in a darkening tone. "Bustin' t' change her will, way I got it."

"That's what she said. You named in that will, Cheeko?"

Morgan's jaw flopped. You'd have thought from the sudden bulge of his stare he might have swallowed what was left of his chew. A second hard look at Ridge's face made him snort. "When owners start leavin' hired hands —"

"Yes or no?"

"By grab, I don't hev —" The segundo, glaring, caught back the rest as if belatedly reminded that more gophers were caught with sugar than shouting. "I can't think what put . . . say — you ain't had a *look* at it hev you?"

Ridge shook his head.

Morgan said, "You reckon someway she found out about Greene — about him not ownin' that Boxed Bell in Florida?"

"Don't seem real likely. They're still going ahead with plans for that wedding."

"She is, mebbe, but what about him? If he's hauled his freight —"

"Look!" Ridge pointed. "Ain't that him coming now?"

XXIV

Both men stepped out.

Greene, pulled up about three yards from the open door, sat peering whimsically down at the pair. "Cat got your tongues?"

Morgan spat.

Ridge grimly said, "You've had that girl half sick with worry."

The man looked astonished. "But I thought . . . hell, I'm sorry about that — been off with Lafe Murgatroyd hunting that lion. Big devil led us a pretty rough chase. Without them dogs . . ." His cornflower stare moved from one to the other. He picked up his reins, saying contritely, "Reckon I better get over there."

Morgan rasped, "Who's lookin' after that spread while you're up here?"

Greene's wheeling head lifted casual stare across a hunched shoulder. Ridge, cutting in, asked: "You in the market for some variscite claims?"

"What kinda claims?"

"Variscite," Ridge said, and held out the rock.

Greene turned it over and tossed it back. "I wouldn't know one mineral chunk from another. If it was cows," he grinned, "you might have a buyer," and rode off toward the house.

Morgan, scowling after him, shifted his chaw to irascibly growl, "Damn fortune huntin' peckerneck! I wouldn't trust that jigger half a inch further'n I could heave a post hole! Suckin' up t' her without a penny in his pockets! Prob'ly been no nearer Lafe Murgatroyd than you hev!"

"We could check on that. You want to do it?"

"You got more time than I hev — can't do it now, anyhow. You forgettin' this is the day we're ridin' in t' record them claims?"

Ridge's glance reached across the yard to encompass Orren Shackleford stepping out of the house. Pausing at gallery's edge he called in their direction, "How about fetching my horse for me, Cheeko?"

Morgan threw up an arm, cursing under his breath, and was wheeling away when Ridge, tramping after him, said, "You go ahead and ride on in with them. I'll join you later."

Morgan slewed a quick look at him. "You goin' over to Lafe's?"

"Kind of thought I might drop by."

"You want I should get them claims fixed up fer you?"

"I'd be obliged," Ridge answered. "If it won't put you out none."

Once away from Tadpole headquarters he set out for town at a pretty good clip. He wasn't overlooking the risk of running into that marshal, but the need to set at rest a couple of matters which had been gnawing at him looked to be worth whatever peril he might encounter. If he kept a sharp lookout he reckoned he could cut it.

Much stronger than his desire to find out if the man calling himself Billy Greene had been spending his time in the brush hunting lions was Ridge's mounting curiosity as to what he'd been figuring to pay for Farley Creek with, had Shackleford agreed to sell it. He couldn't have cared less about the fellow's identity — he might have every right to the name without owning so much as a foot of Boxed Bell. It was the fellow's financial status Ridge was interested in. There was an urgency about this he wasn't minded to put off.

Morgan had the man pegged as a penniless drifter living off his wits but Ridge — every hackle lifted — was determined to get at the truth of the matter; the need to know pushed the pace without care.

By ignoring the road, cutting each corner, he came into Clifton a couple hours past noon, well in advance of the contingent from Tadpole.

He'd have liked, now he thought of it, to have examined Greene's room at the Cliff House, but a little reflection warned him away from it. Dropping out of the saddle he went into the bank and asked for the manager, glad he had thought to scrape his face.

Shown into a cubbyhole room at the back he identified himself as a Sonoita cowman and got down to business. "Billy Greene — he's been living at the Cliff House — wants to buy my spread. I'd be obliged for anything you can tell me about his financial situation."

The manager, showing a frosty smile, declared himself in no position to discuss a depositor's account.

Ridge smiled, too. "I wasn't expecting anything like that. He gave your bank as reference. Does he have an account here?"

The manager considered, finally nodding.

"He's made a commitment to bind the deal but has to come up with another fifteen hundred no later than tomorrow or forfeit the money already put into it. I'd like to know if he can meet that obligation."

"You'll know tomorrow, won't you?"

Ridge grimaced ruefully. "Happens," he said, "I've had another, better offer — substantially better as a matter of fact. Fellow don't want to hold off till tomorrow. He's got a cashier's check on a Ft. Worth bank that appears to be burning a hole in his pocket. I should think you could say whether Greene's in a position —"

"Why not ask the gentleman himself?"

The man's inflection, the twist of his glance, pretty near caused Butler to jerk round in his chair, half expecting to discover Greene behind him. He caught himself in the nick of time. "Would," he growled, "if I could get hold of him. He's not at the hotel — they don't know where he's at."

Eyeing him dubiously the banker diddled a couple breaths longer. "I suppose in that case . . . just a moment," he said and, getting up, left the room, quietly pulling the door shut behind him.

Ridge was half of a mind to haul freight, sweatily wondering if the pasty-faced fellow was sending for the marshal. Way his luck was running it could be in the cards.

He was just pushing up when the manager returned with a smile of apology. "Sorry to have kept you waiting. Looks like you're stuck with it. Mr. Greene has the funds to cover that amount."

Outside, with the sweat standing cold on his neck, Ridge stood a long moment beside his horse, grappling with the fury that was surging inside him. What had started as a hunch was swiftly nearing the proportions of conviction. Without knowing any more than he had just left the bank with, it was dollars to doughnuts the amount in Greene's account coincided to the penny with the money Ridge had lost — that $1,875 dumped on the Cliff House bed by Benton Flores from his carpetbagger's satchel!

Made precious little difference how Billy'd got onto it. Could have been him who'd gone through Ridge's belongings that first night or next morning while he'd been at the livery dickering for that claybank. Greene — in all those hours he had been out of sight — could have had plenty of chance to nip up there and lift it!

Though filled with his anger Ridge had the sense to remind himself that most of the hard thoughts swirling through his head were sprung from that wire Cheeko'd put in his hands.

Building himself up with a cock-and-bull story of owning this big operation in Florida, charming Cora with his hair-brushed good looks and ingratiating smile — or making off, if he had, with the money cached under that Cliff House bureau — was a far piece from proving the kid's only interest in Tadpole's owner lay in what he might get out of her.

There were at least two sides to just about everything, and taking suspicions for gospel, dashing off half cocked, could be exactly what somebody expected him to do.

In plain hard fact what could he prove?

Even that paper Morgan had slipped him . . . every railroad telegrapher and Western Union outpost had pads of them laying round for anyone to take. It was going to need more than a scrap of yellow paper to pin dead wood on a kid smart enough to leave that bunch of rifle wavers holding the sack!

Ridge's first heated impulse to beat the truth out of Billy began to look about as stupid as the half-formed notion the goddam kid was Benny's client.

In the first place Greene didn't have that kind of money. In the second no one who had got this close to what he was after would ever be chump enough pay for the demise of the goose he was counting on to lay his golden eggs! He had to marry the girl if he would get his hands on Tadpole. *But he might very well have latched onto Ridge's nest egg.*

It wasn't the sort of thought to spread much oil on troubled waters; nor was all Ridge's fuming as he swung into saddle inspired to provide a feasible notion as to how he might shake Greene loose of the stake.

Then as he turned his mount between buildings, bound across lots toward the white picket fence that enclosed the judge's residence, he thought again of the telegram Cheeko had shown him and probed his shirt pocket to make sure he still had it. With the paper's reassuring feel in his fingers the glimmer of an idea began to shape up.

Didn't seem likely that, short of getting rough with him, he would get much change from a man of Turlock's caliber. In his present smoldering mood he was not of a mind to brook much resistance.

His knock went unheeded. Pounding again without reply he twisted the knob and, finding it unlocked, invited himself in. Guardedly calling he prowled through rooms till he found the judge's study and a desk stuffed with papers. He was staring at this when Turlock said back of him: "Expect to find me in one of them pigeon-holes?"

"Not rightly," Ridge grunted, turning to face him. "Cora Lee sent me to pick up that will if you've got it ironed out."

"Let's see her note."

"She didn't give me no note."

"Then I guess," Turlock said, "you've had a long ride for nothing. I don't make it a practice of handing over wills without written authorization."

After an exchange of hard looks Ridge said, "Reckon it must have slipped her mind. She tell you why she was making the change?"

"If she did it's no concern of yours," Turlock answered, but Ridge shook his head. "I was hired to protect her —"

"Not against Greene," the judge snapped, off balance, then chewed at his lip, cheeks resentfully darkening as Ridge thinly smiled.

"What's she done — cut him out of his prospects?"

"Get out of my house!" cried Turlock, furious.

Fed up with frustrations Ridge growled,

"Keep that voice down," and — bitterly knowing how far civility would get him — fetched the big six-shooter off his hip.

The old man didn't blanch. "Pegged you right first time I saw you." He looked his contempt.

Nodding, Ridge said, "Thing heavy as this is like to leave some bad wrinkles if I have to work you over. Now dig up that will before I do you a hurt."

"You're surely not fool enough to think you've been named —"

Wondering how hard a rap the old fart could take, Ridge moved toward him lifting the pistol.

"All right," Turlock grumbled, despising himself. "Will's in that next to last hole on the left."

"Shove your chin against that wall and put your mitts up high as you can get 'em," Ridge ordered and, soon as the judge was where he wanted him, yanked all the papers from the indicated pigeonhole. It took no time at all to find what he was after. A swift look confirmed his hunch — there was no mention whatever of Billy Greene. For 'loyal service' Morgan was named to receive twelve hundred.

Ridge tossed the document back with the others. "You can turn around now.

What'd she take out?"

Turlock's jaws were stubbornly clamped.

"All right. Read this." Ridge handed him the wire from the Florida marshal.

The judge put on his spectacles, glanced at it briefly and handed it back. "Surprised you had the gall to get in touch with —"

" 'Fore she made this change I reckon she left Billy the whole shebang. He leave that Boxed Bell outfit to her?"

"The two of them came here together. Made identical wills."

"Only now it seems he'd nothing to will her. You know if she's told him what she's done?"

"Said she was going to."

"Strike you she was scared of the feller?"

The judge said grudgingly, "Expect they'd had some kind of squabble. She appeared more riled than anything else." His voice toughened up. "You'll not get away with this —"

Ridge, grinning, took a short turning stride and jabbed a finger hard against Turlock's chest. "You better hope I do if you care anything at all about C. L. Kelly. Somebody wants that girl plumb dead."

XXV

Back in the saddle Ridge couldn't rightly see what to do next. Leaving Turlock loose to run off at the mouth probably wasn't either sensible or healthy. Way this was going, about the healthiest notion that crossed his mind was to head for the border by the shortest route. But he curled his lip. He'd come into this deal to pile up a stake and leaving empty-handed was no cure for anything.

Tomorrow was the day set for Cora Lee's wedding and, in view of the work she had just put the judge to, he couldn't help wondering if she honestly meant to go through with it. Why cut Greene out of her will if she figured on spending the rest of her life with him? Yes, and what about *him?* If he'd been setting the bag to lay hold of that property where was the good of marrying her now? Was it possible he didn't yet know what she'd done? Or did he hope by sweet talking . . .

A startling thought stuck its claws in Ridge then, so neatly embracing all the disparate elements he could pretty near hear the bits fall in place, like the clicking of tumblers with the right combination.

He forced himself to take a long hard look at it, abruptly heeling his horse toward town.

Suppose Greene in his hunt for a fast buck had stumbled onto that variscite. If the green rock was back of his courtship of Cora, being named to inherit was the crux of his scheming. Securely on record as the girl's legal heir he'd no need to be burdened with any back-country wife the law would hold entitled to half of everything he had. Accept this much and the ten-day deadline given Ridge by Benny made the strongest kind of sense, coinciding exactly with the date Cora'd set for consummation of their nuptials!

But was Billy that coldblooded? Was he slick enough to convincingly court her while planning her destruction? Did he have the sort of guts to bring off such a coup?

Recalling the night they'd gone searching for Cora, the bunch that had jumped them just short of the creek, and the promptness with which Greene had heated his axles Ridge scowlingly nodded, lips grimly thinning at the dexterity with which the kid had got himself clear.

It all hung together well enough, except that . . . where could the kid have managed to scare up the twenty-five hundred handed to Benny to insure the girl's death? Cut it any way you liked, the only man in the picture who might readily put his mitts on that kind of money was Anchor Bar's owner. Friend Orren.

He cut round to ride past the ornate structure housing the county offices without seeing any Tadpole mounts. Since they'd have to come here to record those claims he judged they hadn't yet reached town. Maybe they'd stopped off to feed their faces. Negotiating the twists of the crooked street he presently swung down to step into a saloon, feeling by this time the need to wet his whistle.

Lingering over a mug of warm beer, he had a boot on the rail near the bar's far corner adjacent to a window overlooking the street when a wizened little hombre with a butt in his mouth and a ten-gallon hat on the back of his head shoved through the batwings, snatched a quick look around, made a bee-line for the solitary drinker ensconced at a table and grabbed hold of his shoulder. "Lafe, by Gawd! Had a hunch I'd prob'ly run into you here — that pack of hounds handy?"

"Sure. Got five in each pocket," the seated man snorted.

"How soon can you git 'em out to Hyde's Corners?"

While the drinker at the table pawed at flushed cheeks Ridge, packing his mug, hauled out a chair and, dropping into it, asked, "You Murgatroyd?"

Two pairs of eyes looked him over without welcome. The cigar smoker, glowering, allowed they weren't conducting a caucus. "Get lost," Ridge said with mouth turned thin.

Above swelling chest the fellow's belligerence took a widening look at that half-shut stare and, visibly paler, wheeled away. Shifting his glance to the other, Ridge asked: "Billy Greene with you when you went after that cat for Cheeko Morgan?"

"So what if he was?"

"Just curious, friend. Understand you been around here a spell. What do you call to mind about Spaulding?"

The drink-bleared eyes weighed Ridge again. "You packin' a badge?"

"Not hardly, friend."

"What's your angle?"

"Kin of mine. Been some suggestion he got a dirty deal."

"Bit off more'n he could chew is all.

Knew the odds when he bought Farley Creek — *had* t' know, damn it! Got it for a song. Figgered to be tougher than the upshot warranted. Been plenty others tried t' paddle that boat. My advice t' you is forgit it."

"That sounds like a man with a grievance."

The dog man took another pull at his rotgut. "Why you reckon I piddle round chasin' these cats? Had me a spread in this country once — six years now it's been a Anchor Bar line-camp."

"Which camp is that?"

"Last stop short of Tadpole."

"Orren buy you out?"

Murgatroyd's laugh was an ugly sound. "That's what the books show."

Ridge stood up. "I'm obliged," he growled, and dropped a bill on the table. "Have a bottle on me."

It was cooler outside, but not very much. Ridge lounged at the rack by the head of his horse, scanning the traffic from beneath the down-tugged brim of his hat.

Tiny white clouds like puffs of smoke motionlessly hung against the glare of sky but Ridge's quartering stare hardly noticed; he was looking for Orren and Cora and Morgan and wondering where the damned marshal was at as the strain of this business began to take hold of him.

He didn't figure it too likely him and that badge-packer would run into each other with the place so filled with all these comings and goings, but the chance kept him edgy. One second of carelessness could get a man planted.

Abruptly his glance picked up Shackleford shoving through people to get into the bank. Ridge next spotted Morgan and Cora sitting their mounts beside Orren's horse. As the dust of a passing freight rig thinned he spied Billy Greene — likewise mounted — knee round the horn and a look on his mug you'd not think to find on the face of a man so nearly a bridegroom.

Coming up to them Ridge remarked, "Buck up, kid. Eve of a marriage's supposed to be a time for joyful noises —"

"We're not getting married," Cora said shortly, and Greene's jaw dropped as Ridge swung a look at her.

"Allowed you reckoned the sun rose and set in him."

A deeper color spread through her cheeks but she fetched up her chin in that remembered defiance and, holding his stare, declared with an appalling frankness, "I thought so, too . . . until you came along. Oh, there was probably more to it

— fright anyway. I felt different around you . . . safer someway. I seemed to begin to sense in Billy —"

"What the devil!" Greene said. "You throwing me over for this gun toting drifter?"

She peered at him thoughtfully. "I think you'll survive." She brought her gaze back to Ridge. "I began to sense in him certain inconsistencies that confused and disturbed me . . . little things —"

With sudden heat Greene snapped, "I don't have to listen to that kind of guff!" and was wheeling his mount in a scowl of temper when Ridge reached out and caught hold of its cheek-strap.

"What's your rush? Guy with a broken heart should look crushed, not go flyin' off in a half-assed tantrum. You've still got chips in this. Set a while, Billy."

With them all looking at him Greene uncomfortably shrugged, angry glance swiveling across Morgan's hunched shoulder to pick up Orren Shackleford coming out of the bank.

The rancher, rejoining them, flashed a hard look at Ridge and got into his saddle. "Let's get this over with," he growled gruffly at Cora, and kneed his horse out into the traffic. The girl and Morgan

213

turned their mounts after him and Ridge told Greene, "You're next," sitting there motionless until the kid sullenly moved his roan in behind them.

This was not a time for any mistakes. He kept a good ten feet between himself and Greene's roan, narrowly watching both of the others, alert for the first fledgling hint of trouble, hand hanging loose by the butt of his pistol.

Coming up on the building which housed the county offices he dropped back a bit more, watching the others get out of saddle before he swung down. Orren hustled inside, Morgan hard on his heels. Midway on the steps Greene twisted his neck for a backward look, face furrowing nastily when Ridge motioned him on.

"Listen —" Billy cried, both feet planted stubbornly, "what the hell is there in there for me? You heard what she said —"

"Trot along, Billy."

"Damned if I will!"

Ridge's eyes rimmed with frost. "Don't lay your character down out here. Be no handy limb for you to grab this trip."

The kid appeared to get a little pale around the gills. With those rolling eyes it almost seemed for a couple of breaths he was minded to kick clean over the traces.

Ridge smiled with his teeth. Some of the wildness leached from Greene's face. With a snarl he followed the others inside.

It was Morgan's face that now caught Ridge's notice. They were all huddled round the clerk at the counter and the black-patched range boss looked like a man on the verge of apoplexy. With a half-strangled shout he made a grab for his iron but Ridge caught the wrist before he could lift it. "No call for gunplay."

"No call!" Cheeko yelled. "You know what that mealy-mouthed son of a bitch done?" His eyes blazed at Cora's erstwhile affinity. *"Snuk in here yesterday an' recorded every goddam one of them claims!"*

Ridge glanced from Shackleford's obvious amusement past the compassionate understanding in the girl's expression to the frantic shape of the man who'd declared there was nothing for him here. From livid cheeks Greene hoarsed in a sort of forlorn desperation, "I only done it for *her!* Trying to protect the stupid bitch —"

"Lemme at 'im!" Morgan panted, struggling. Ridge, twisting the six-shooter out of his grip, stepped back to say, "I'd bet on that, Billy. And no time like the present to make sure you didn't run your tail off for nothing. Get a quitclaim deed and a pen

215

from this feller and let's see how quick you can get 'em made over to her."

Outrage blazed from the kid's bitter stare; but when the clerk fetched the requisites there was little, in that atmosphere, he could do but oblige. Flinging down the pen he was wheeling to leave when he ran head-on into an unyielding stiffness.

The bore of Morgan's pistol dug deeper into his midriff. "You ain't done with this yet. Should be some kinda hereafter for a skunk who'd scheme the demise of his betrothed, then to make doubly sure take a whack at her himself."

Dissonant sounds from the street outside grew surprisingly clear in the ugly quiet. Greene licked at his lips with a scratchy tongue. An embarrassing stain began to seep down a pantsleg and his jumpety stare jerked to single out Shackleford. Before anything else could get itself said, Cora Lee cried, "Why don't you just let the pipsqueak go?"

Benny's contract man took a long look at Orren. It didn't seem to matter much who'd actually put up the money. Ridge grabbed a fresh breath. "Reckon I could manage to live with that . . . long as you're about to be Mrs. Ridge Butler."